QUAKE!

DISASTER IN
SAN FRANCISCO, 1906

Gail Langer Karwoski

Illustrated by
Robert Papp

PEACHTREE
ATLANTA

Ω

Published by
PEACHTREE PUBLISHERS, LTD.
1700 Chattahoochee Avenue
Atlanta, Georgia 30318

www.peachtree-online.com

Text © 2004 by Gail Langer Karwoski
Illustrations © 2004 by Robert Papp

First trade paperback edition published January 2006

Photographs courtesy of *www.sfmuseum.org*

Cover design by Loraine M. Joyner
Book design by Melanie McMahon Ives

Manufactured in the United States of America

10 9 8 7 6 5 4 3   (hardcover)
10 9 8 7 6 5 4 3 2   (paperback)

Library of Congress Cataloging-in-Publication Data

Karwoski, Gail, 1949–
    Quake / by Gail Langer Karwoski ; illustrated by Robert Papp.-- 1st ed.
       p. cm.
    Summary: Tells the story of the 1906 San Francisco earthquake as seen through the eyes of Jacob, a thirteen-year-old Jewish boy who lives in a boarding house with his father and younger sister.
    ISBN 1-56145-310-2
    ISBN 1-56145-369-2
    1.   Earthquakes--California--San Francisco--Juvenile fiction. [1. Earthquakes--California--San Francisco--Fiction. 2. Jews--United States--Fiction. 3. San Francisco (Calif.)--History--20th century--Fiction. 4. Immigrants--Fiction. 5. Dogs--Fiction.] I. Papp, Robert, ill. II. Title.

    PZ7.K153Qu 2003
    [Fic]--dc22
                                    2003020627

*For my daughter Leslie,
who turned nine in San Francisco
and loves the city's spirit as much as I do.*

—GLK

TABLE OF CONTENTS

CHAPTER 1
APRIL 17, 1906

At first he didn't notice the dog. Late afternoon sun bathed the cobblestones as Jacob Kaufman trudged up Washington Street to finish the deliveries from his father's meat stand. On such an unusually warm April day, the bustling streets of downtown San Francisco should have been a delight for a boy of thirteen. But since his mother's death, Jacob hardly noticed his surroundings. His mind was blanketed by troubling thoughts, like the fog that sometimes blew in from the bay and blocked out the sky.

Something bumped against Jacob's leg, and he stopped and looked down. It was a young dog with a springy step and golden brown fur. Jacob had never seen a dog carry its tail like this one, curled into a perfect letter C over its rump.

Jacob watched the dog nose a grape that had fallen on the ground. The animal licked the little fruit, then tried to pick it up with its teeth, but the grape rolled into the dirt between the cobblestones. Eyes alert and muscles tense, the dog pounced. When the grape wedged in a hole, the dog began to paw at it, but the lumpy stones stuck up too far. Frustrated, the dog made a sound that was part whine, part howl.

Jacob picked up the sticky, grit-covered grape and held it out on his palm. The dog opened its mouth in what looked like a grin and wagged its tail. Taking a cautious step toward Jacob, it nuzzled the boy's palm, then enclosed the grape in its sparkling white teeth. Instead of biting down, the dog rolled the rubbery grape around in its mouth, tilting its head from side to side. Finally the puzzled dog spit the unbroken grape onto the street and sniffed it curiously.

Laughing out loud, Jacob petted the animal's soft head. The dog twisted its mouth into that odd little grin again.

"Tell you what, fella," Jacob said. "You probably wouldn't like that grape even if you could figure out how to eat it. Try this instead." He reached into his sack and tore a greasy chunk of fat off the meat inside. The dog gulped down the fat, then licked Jacob's fingers until every trace of grease was gone.

"What's going on here?" boomed Uncle Avram. "I ask my brother the butcher to send me some meat for supper, and here my nephew is giving it away to a stray dog?"

Jacob looked up. Avram Kaufman's big hands were planted on his narrow hips and the muscles in his arms bulged beneath his rolled-up sleeves. Although he spoke in a loud, stern voice, his dark eyes sparkled with laughter.

Jacob grinned at his uncle as he stood up and handed over the sack.

Avram was the younger of the two Kaufman brothers. Short and slim, he had dark, curly hair and a good-natured if homely face—unruly eyebrows, thick nose, and fleshy lips. Jacob called him Uncle Avi, and his uncle's deep, hearty laugh was what he always associated with the man.

Avi tousled Jacob's hair and asked, "How goes it at my brother's home, nephew?"

Suddenly the fog seemed to wrap around Jacob's mind again. *Home.* Jacob pictured the dark boardinghouse south of Mission Street where he and his father and sister lived. He could practically smell the familiar odors—cabbage boiling on the stove,

"What's going on here?" boomed Uncle Avram.

latkes sizzling in the pan. With the memory, Jacob felt an ache deep inside, an indescribable longing and emptiness. *Oh, Uncle Avi,* Jacob wanted to say, *there's no such thing as a home without a mother!*

"All right, I guess," Jacob mumbled, avoiding his uncle's eyes. He knew that if he tried to describe his feelings, his uncle would stare at him with eyes full of pity. Then Jacob's voice would crack, and he was afraid he'd start crying like a baby. He would not let himself cry. Not in front of his uncle—and certainly not in front of strangers on a public street. On Jacob's last birthday he had celebrated his Bar Mitzvah. So in the eyes of his Jewish forefathers, wasn't he already a man?

Avi shifted his weight from one foot to the other. "I see you've made friends with this little dog," he said. "He's a foolish animal, don't you think? A dog that comes begging on the street of the fruit and vegetable peddlers. Wouldn't you think his nose would lead him to the street of the butchers? Or to the wharves, where fishermen bring in their catch?"

"Maybe he belongs to one of the peddlers?"

Uncle Avi shook his head. "He belongs to nobody, Jacob. And how do I know this? Because for three days and three nights, this foolish animal follows me around like he's my shadow. I ignore him, but he follows me anyway. So last night I take pity on him and bring out a little bowl of scraps for him to eat. And what do you think he does? He gobbles them up so fast that I'm afraid he's going to choke, like he hasn't eaten in a month!"

Jacob smiled and leaned over to stroke the dog's velvety ears. "So this dog does belong to somebody, Uncle Avi. He belongs to you."

"Nah!" Avi exclaimed, waving his hand through the air. "What am I going to do with a dog? What am I going to feed him? Apple peels? And your Aunt Rose—don't even ask! She let me have it! When I came back in the house, Rose grabbed the empty bowl and started hollering. 'What do you think you're doing, Avram Kaufman? We have three babies to feed, and all of a sudden you decide to bring home stray dogs—Noo! Is this what I need?' She yelled so loud I thought my ears would burst!"

Jacob grinned. Most of the Jews who had moved from Poland to San Francisco—like his father and uncle—knew one another. Among them, Rose Kaufman had a reputation. Everybody said her tongue was sharper than a butcher's knife. Over the years, Jacob had often heard his parents discussing Aunt Rose. Mamma used to defend her sister-in-law by saying that Rose "means well." But Papa always replied, "Rose has a mouth as big as a whale, and who worries about what a whale means as it swallows you?"

"Rose says she has enough to do, with an infant to nurse and twins still in diapers," Avi continued. "She told me if I wanted to share my home with a stray dog, I could take my blanket out to the street and use my cart for my bed and a bunch of bananas as my pillow!"

"So what will you do with the dog?" Jacob asked.

Avi rubbed his chin. "I don't know," he said. "I thought maybe I would ask your father if he wants a dog…for his children to play with. Maybe a dog would take their minds off their sorrow."

Jacob's dark eyebrows shot up. "Really?"

Avi nodded.

Jacob knelt and scratched the white fur on the dog's chin and chest. The dog made that odd little grinning face and wiggled its whole body. Then it licked Jacob's eyelids. Jacob rolled the dog onto its back and scratched its dirty belly until the animal wriggled with pleasure.

As he played with the dog, Jacob glanced at his uncle. A smile lit up Avi's face, and Jacob guessed what his uncle was thinking. "You look just like I remember your father looked when he was a boy," Avi always said. "The same black, curly hair. The same skinny arms and long fingers, even the same laugh." Whenever they sat around the table at family gatherings, Avi told stories about the Kaufman brothers' childhood, about all the times they got into mischief playing on the muddy paths of their village in Poland.

Avi put his hand on his nephew's head. "Now remember, I haven't spoken to your father yet," he said. "So don't get attached to this dog. Itzak may not like the idea. He may think a dog would only be more trouble. After all, your sister Sophie is too little to take care of a pet. And you're busy delivering meat as soon as you come home from school."

"But the dog could stay in the house with Sophie. Then she wouldn't be so frightened of staying by herself."

Avi winced and chewed his lip. "A five-year-old is too young to stay home by herself, even with a dog. I told your father that my Rose will watch over Sophie. As soon as the baby starts sleeping a little better, Rose promised me that she'll watch over your sister while Itzak is at work."

"Well, then the dog could stay at Papa's meat stand until I get home from school. In the afternoon, I can take him with me while I do the deliveries," Jacob said. He was getting more excited as he talked. "Look! He's not such a big dog—he won't eat so much. Besides, Papa is a butcher—he has plenty of scraps, fat and bones. He gives them away to poor families whenever they ask, and still he has more that he throws away."

"Jacob, Jacob, you're always full of answers!" Avi laughed. "But it's for Itzak to decide, so don't get your heart set."

Jacob's smile faded. He stood and brushed off his pants.

"You're right, Uncle Avi. I know what my father will say. 'No.' That's what he says about everything. He'll say that he's got enough trouble, with a son who does nothing but daydream. And a five-year-old daughter who has no mother to watch over her. He'll say he doesn't need another headache, like a dog."

Avi put his hand on Jacob's shoulder. "Itzak loved your mother very much, you know. It's not easy for him."

Jacob pulled away. "I have to go, Uncle Avi," he said. "Sophie is all by herself, and you know how scared she is of staying alone when it gets dark. It'll take me at least a half hour to get home, even if I run most of the way."

"Wait a minute, nephew!" Avi said. "I want you to tell my brother something…" He paused, thinking, then spoke rapidly. "Tell Itzak that he should bring Sophie to my house tomorrow morning. So Rose can watch over her."

"But Uncle Avi," Jacob objected, "you just told me that Aunt Rose can't take care of Sophie until the new baby—"

"Why are you telling me what Rose can or cannot do?" Avi scolded. "Who is married to your Aunt Rose—you or me? I say that Rose is ready to watch Sophie! Isn't Sophie the only daughter of my only brother? Of course the aunt should watch the niece!" Avi slapped his hands up and down as though he had just unloaded a dusty carton and he was brushing off his palms.

"In return," Avi added, "my brother should take this dog off my hands. Tell Itzak that if he doesn't, he will be forcing his younger brother to sleep outside. With a bunch of bananas for a pillow."

Jacob grinned. "Are you sure, Uncle Avi?"

"Of course I'm sure." He took Jacob by the shoulders. "Now you go home. You shouldn't leave Sophie all alone when it's about to get dark. Take this dog with you. You tell my brother that a dog should not have to eat apple peels for the rest of its life. And here in America, children should not have to eat misery for the rest of their lives."

As Jacob turned to go, Avi grabbed the boy's head and hugged it to his chest. "I would come to tell my brother these things myself, but I have something else to do this evening. I have to go to the flower peddler and see if he has any roses to sell."

Avi winked at his nephew. "You know, Jacob, when I bring roses to my wife, I always remove the thorns and throw them away. I do this so my children will not get scratched." Avi nodded as he continued. "Tonight I will explain to your Aunt Rose that I do this because I am the father, and I want the children to be safe. I am also the uncle to you and Sophie. It is my duty to make sure all the children in the family are safe."

Jacob laughed. Then he slapped his thigh, and the dog bounded to his side. He backed away, watching the dog follow with that odd little grin on its whiskered face. Waving good-bye to his uncle, he turned to go. As he ran down the hill the dog ran beside him, pink tongue hanging out of one side of its mouth.

CHAPTER 2

A HOUSE BUT NOT A HOME

A steady stream of horse-drawn wagons rattled through the streets, forcing Jacob to stop at every corner until the traffic passed. Each time he stopped, the dog sat down beside his leg. As soon as Jacob stepped onto the street the dog jumped up and trotted along beside him.

Downtown was jammed with people rushing to get home at the end of the workday. Men wearing dark suits and round derby hats hurried by with newspapers tucked under their arms, their polished shoes clomping on the cobblestones. A woman bustled past, carrying a cloth-covered basket on her arm. Jacob's stomach grumbled as he caught a whiff of fresh bread from her basket.

On Market Street a cable car conductor waved and Jacob waved back. Glancing up and down the busy thoroughfare, he could see City Hall on his right. A dome crowned the top of this famous building, and a smaller onion-shaped dome perched on its very top. Across the building's entranceway, a row of tall columns stood as straight as soldiers, and more columns guarded its second and third stories. Papa said City Hall was the biggest building in California and as fancy as a palace—proof that San Francisco was one of the most prosperous cities in America.

QUAKE

Just south of Market Street, Jacob stopped to watch a row of automobiles—each one polished to a gleam—gliding down the street. He guessed the well-dressed passengers sitting in the rear seats of those shiny cars were on their way to the Grand Opera House. Jacob had seen handbills advertising tonight's event all over town. Everybody had heard of the show's star, Enrico Caruso, the world-famous tenor. Caruso's name was printed on the handbills in even larger letters than *Carmen,* the title of the opera.

Of course, Jacob had never been to a show at the Grand Opera House, or, for that matter, any stage show. He had certainly never ridden in an automobile.

But who knows what tomorrow may bring? he thought, echoing one of his father's favorite expressions. Before Mamma died, Papa always used to talk about how lucky they were to live in America, a country full of opportunities.

Papa no longer gushed with such enthusiasm, but Jacob felt it now. Here he was, walking home with a dog—the first pet he'd ever owned. *Wait 'til Sophie sees!* Jacob chuckled as he imagined his little sister's eyes opening wide with surprise.

After crossing Mission Street, Jacob was about five blocks from home. He fairly flew up Howard Street, where wooden boardinghouses of two, three, and four stories stood so close together that their walls nearly touched. In this neighborhood, people streamed in and out of every doorway. Children skipped and played. Women carried bags stuffed full of merchandise purchased from shops along the street.

Colorful signs hung above each shop front, and their windows displayed all kinds of goods—leather boots and bins full of olives, hammers and ladies' hats, wheels of cheese and square bars of soap. The dog held its nose high and sniffed the air. Jacob breathed deeply, taking in the spicy aroma of cooking food that drifted from open apartment windows, the earthy smell of horse dung on the street, and the sour odor of damp cellars.

He nodded a greeting to a girl from his school. The dog wagged its tail as they hurried by a group of younger boys who were shooting marbles in front of one doorway. Jacob shouted hello to Mr. Straussberg, the owner of the cobbler shop in the building two doors from his house.

Just ahead of him, Jacob saw an old woman carrying some large bundles toward the Nevada Boarding House. Although he'd never met her, Jacob recognized her as Timothy O'Connor's grandmother. Jacob was in such a good mood, he felt like doing a kindness for someone. So he caught up to the old woman and introduced himself as a classmate of her grandson. Then he offered to carry her bundles up the stairs.

"Why no, I'll not be needin' yer assistance, lad," Mrs. O'Connor answered. "I'm thankin' ye for the offer, though." She stopped at the doorway. "I'm pleased to make yer acquaintance. Jacob, ye said yer name is?"

"Yes, ma'am. Jacob Kaufman. The butcher's son," Jacob answered. "Timothy and I have been in the same class for two years."

"I'll be sure and tell Timmy what a nice young man ye are," said Mrs. O'Connor with a wink. She made a clicking noise with her lips, and the dog perked up its ears. "And don't ye have a sweet dog there? I can tell ye take good care of yer little pet."

Jacob beamed and said good-bye to Mrs. O'Connor. He turned into the dark wooden boardinghouse next door. As soon as he opened the front door, the familiar smells of the old building greeted him: the heavy aroma of simmering stewpots hung over the stale odor of sweat and grime. The dog hesitated, then squeezed past Jacob and began sniffing the dusty staircase.

Jacob whistled softly, and the two of them bounded up the steps.

When they reached the fourth floor, Jacob picked up the dog and tiptoed down the hall so he could surprise Sophie. He rapped sharply on the door of their apartment. After a long pause, he heard a small voice: "Jacob? Is that you?"

Jacob spoke in a stern tone. "Sophie, you did it again! How many times do I have to remind you? You're supposed to pretend that nobody is there. If it's me, I'll open the door and let myself in. It's not safe to let strangers know a little girl is at home alone. I'm going to have to tell Papa on you!"

"I forgot, Jacob," the voice whined. "Don't tell Papa," she pleaded. "Pleeeease."

The door opened slowly, and Sophie looked up at her brother. Her eyes became as round as bagels when she saw what Jacob was holding.

Jacob put the squirming dog on the floor and watched it wiggle up to Sophie, grinning and batting its tail. Sophie backed up, frightened. The dog sat down in front of her, tail swabbing the floorboards, and let out a whining howl.

Jacob shut the door behind him. "Don't be afraid, Sophie."

Sophie gingerly held out one small hand, and the dog licked her fingers.

"I found him on Washington Street," Jacob explained. "Uncle Avi told me to take him home with me. He said Aunt Rose would make him sleep on the street if he kept the dog."

Sophie took a step closer and touched the soft fur on the animal's back. The dog's face screwed up into that odd little grin, then it flopped down and rolled onto its back, legs poking in the air.

"Go ahead and rub his tummy, Sophie," Jacob urged. "He won't hurt you."

When Sophie touched the dog's belly, the animal wiggled and

squirmed. Suddenly it flipped over and mopped the girl's face with his tongue.

Sophie exploded into giggles. "He's kissing me! The doggy's kissing me!" Sophie squeezed her eyes shut and turned her head away. The dog licked Sophie's ear and nosed her dark ringlets. "He tickles!" Sophie squealed with joy. "Jacob, the doggy's tickling me!"

Sophie clamped her shoulder against her damp ear and ran behind her brother. The dog followed.

"Look, Jacob!" she said. "The doggy likes me!" Sophie dropped to her knees and hugged the dog's head. "Where did Uncle Avi get him?" she asked.

Before Jacob could answer, Sophie asked another question. "Is he a boy dog or a girl dog? Oh, what a good doggy! Look, Jacob, his tongue is pink! Do you see the doggy's pink tongue?"

"Slow down, Sophie, I can't answer all your questions at the same time!" Jacob crouched beside his sister and slapped the floorboards. The dog sprang into the air. Jacob slapped the floor again, and the dog raced around the room, tongue hanging out of one side of its mouth.

Sophie twirled around and around, watching. She giggled, clapped her hands, and jumped up and down. Jacob hadn't seen his sister laugh like this in months.

At last the dog slid to a stop, and Jacob scratched its chin. Sophie slumped against her brother's shoulder. "I'm hungry," she said, slipping her thumb into her mouth. Taking Sophie's hand, Jacob led her to the table and broke off a piece of bread for her. The dog sat beside Sophie's chair, following Jacob with eager eyes.

"I know," Jacob said to the dog, "you're hungry, too."

"What's the doggy's name, Jacob?" Sophie asked as she stuffed half of her bread into her mouth and handed the other half to the dog. It gulped down the bread and looked at Sophie for more.

"I don't know," Jacob said. "Uncle Avi didn't call him by any name. I guess we can name him whatever we want."

"Let's call him Fluffy," Sophie said. "Or Spotty."

"The dog's fur is short, Sophie. Not fluffy. And he doesn't have spots. We should name him something that describes him." Jacob took three potatoes from a basket on the floor and started peeling them.

"But I like the name Fluffy," Sophie whined. "And the doggy's—"

At the sound of heavy footsteps on the stairs, Sophie looked toward the door. "Papa's home!"

"Sophie, wait!" Jacob cried.

But he was too late. Sophie slid off her chair and rushed to open the door. "Look, Papa," she shouted, "a doggy! Jacob brought a doggy!"

Itzak Kaufman was taller and leaner than his brother Avi, and his black hair was sprinkled with gray above his ears. A butcher's apron, smeared with reddish brown stains, covered his shirt and pants. He held a small sack in his hand.

Jacob watched his father's deep-set, dark eyes fasten on the dog. Before the man uttered a single word, Jacob knew that he was not going to agree to keep the dog. Itzak patted Sophie's head. Looking at Jacob, he nodded toward the dog and raised one bushy eyebrow.

The dog whined softly and edged close to Jacob's knee.

"Uncle Avi gave him to me," Jacob blurted out. "He's a stray. He's been following Uncle Avi around for days, and Aunt Rose is having fits. She said—" Jacob stopped. He'd meant to tell his father the good news first, about how his uncle was going to insist that his wife watch Sophie. "Uncle Avi says you should bring Sophie to his house tomorrow. Aunt Rose is going to watch her while you go to work."

Itzak nodded and put the sack on the table. When he began to speak, his tone was even. "Jacob, we cannot—"

"But, Papa, Uncle Avi says you'll be repaying him by taking the dog. If he keeps it, Rose will kick him out of the house. He says that he has only apple peels to feed a dog, but a dog shouldn't have to eat apple peels for the rest of its life. And since you're a butcher, it wouldn't be any problem for us to feed him. This dog really won't be any trouble, Papa. When I walked home from the Produce District, he—"

"Jacob," Itzak held up his hand to halt his son's avalanche of words. "You're old enough in the eyes of the world to be a man. So you're old enough to show a little sense. What are we going to do with a dog in this tiny apartment? Don't we have enough problems trying to take care of Sophie, now that your mother is..." Itzak's voice cracked, and he turned away.

After taking a deep breath, Itzak began again. "Look, son," he said gently, "someday we'll move into a better place. Sophie will be a bigger girl. Then we'll think about things like having a pet. Not now. It hasn't even been four months since we lost your mother."

"But Papa—" Jacob protested.

"Jacob, did you hear me?"

Jacob could feel his face getting hot. "Yes, I heard you. But I don't think the—"

"Silence!" Itzak commanded. "I said *no*. The father has spoken. No means no. Better you should pay attention to your schoolwork than waste time with a dog." Itzak's voice became quieter. "You know, Jacob, when I was your age, I—"

"I don't care what happened when you were my age!" Jacob shouted. He heard Sophie whimper, but he didn't stop. "You lived in Poland, but I live here in America. Things are different here. Even Uncle Avi says that children are not supposed to be unhappy all the time."

Sophie's whimper became a wail. Whenever Jacob and Papa shouted at each other—and that was almost every day in the last couple of months—Sophie cried as if someone was sticking pins in her.

"Hush, Sophie," Itzak snapped, "before the neighbors start complaining again."

Sophie made a great effort to swallow her cries. She sniffled, then took a deep, ragged breath.

The dog crept closer to Jacob and cowered behind his legs. Frightened, the animal quivered all over like an egg in a pot of boiling water.

Itzak slumped onto the only padded chair in the apartment and pulled off his heavy shoes. "Since when does Avi decide what's best for my children?" he muttered. "Since when is he in charge of this family? Does Avi know what it is to have children with no mother to care for them? Does he know what it is to have a son old enough to be a man, but so idiotic that he brings home stray animals? Who knows what kind of filth and diseases this dog may have?"

Jacob slammed a pan onto the stove and lit the fire under the burner. He grabbed the sack his father had left on the table and emptied it into the pan. As he balled up the sack and threw it on the floor, he stabbed at the small slab of meat with a fork.

Itzak glowered at his son. "Stop it, Jacob! Right now, before you ruin our supper. I ask you, is this the way a Jewish boy behaves? We cannot even take care of your sister by ourselves anymore—we must beg Avi's bad-tempered wife to look after her. And now you want something else to take care of?" Itzak pointed at the dog. "Look! You can see this is not a healthy animal. It's shaking all over, like it has a fever. That's all I need—

a sick dog. Take the dog out to the street and leave it there. Go! Before it makes us all sick."

"No, Papa!" Sophie cried. "Please don't put the doggy outside. It's dark out there. How will the doggy find its mamma in the dark?"

Itzak hesitated, and Jacob saw the muscle in his father's jaw flex. Quietly Jacob reached for the bowl of peeled potatoes and added them to the pan where the meat was browning. *Maybe Papa will change his mind because Sophie is getting upset.*

After a few minutes, his father spoke again. His voice was even, but Jacob knew he was still angry. "The dog can stay here tonight. But he is not to sleep with Sophie. If she gets sick, Rose won't want her in the same house with her babies. Tomorrow morning, the dog goes. Is that clear, Jacob?"

Jacob said nothing.

"Don't be sad, Jacob," Sophie said. "We can see the doggy at Uncle Avi's house."

"Uncle Avi can't keep him," Jacob mumbled.

"So where will the doggy live?" Sophie said, her voice becoming high and shrill again.

"Somebody will take the dog," Itzak said. He held out his arms for Sophie to come to him. The little girl climbed into his lap and put her head on his shoulder while he gently patted her back. When Jacob said the food was ready, Itzak carried Sophie to her chair and placed a plate in front of her.

"Papa, none of the peddlers wants the dog," Jacob said as he took a seat at the table. "If I put him back on the street, he'll starve or get run over. He's not sick. He only started trembling when you came home. He's scared of you."

Sophie put down her fork. "Will the doggy get run over, Papa?"

"The dog will be fine," Itzak said calmly. He turned to Jacob and shot him a warning glance.

"Will somebody take the doggy home?" Sophie asked.

"Of course," Itzak said. "Nothing bad will happen to the dog. Tomorrow morning before school, Jacob will take it back to the Produce District. The dog probably belongs to one of the peddlers."

"He doesn't, Papa," Jacob said. "Uncle Avi said—"

"Jacob, that's enough!" Itzak roared. "Avram is not the head of this family. I am! And my answer is no. We have enough worries without a dog. I don't want to hear another word about it."

Jacob took a mouthful of meat, but it stuck in his throat. He pushed his plate away.

"There's plenty of fat in the pan to feed the dog, son. You're a growing boy and you need to eat. I forbid you to waste your supper on a dog."

Jacob didn't answer. He gave his father the angriest look he could manage and clenched his fists under the table.

"Did you hear me, Jacob?"

Jacob glared.

"Jacob!" Itzak shouted.

"I'm not hungry," Jacob said, his voice sullen.

Sophie looked from her brother to her father, and her lips began to quiver. Jacob knew his father would really go into a rage if she started to wail again, so he grabbed a chunk of bread and stuffed it into his mouth. He chewed mechanically.

At last supper was over. While Itzak got Sophie ready for bed, Jacob fed the scraps to the dog. He watched the animal gulp the meat, then lick up the grease. *Better enjoy this food while you can, fella,* he thought. *Tomorrow you'll be out on the streets, and who knows what will happen to you then.*

Jacob blinked back tears, determined not to let his father catch him crying. *He'll tell me I'm acting like an idiot again. But I'm not the one who starts hollering whenever anybody tries to make a suggestion!*

Gathering the dirty dishes, Jacob let his mind dwell on all the terrible things he wanted to say. *Look at this dump! My father thinks he's such a genius. If he's so smart, why do we live in such a place? But what do I know about anything? I just happen to be the man's son.*

Does he ever listen when I make a suggestion? Oh, no, I'm the idiot, I should keep my mouth shut. Of course, when he needs something done, then he's nice to me. When it comes time to do his deliveries every day, suddenly he treats me like I'm a man. Then he remembers I've had my Bar Mitzvah. Sure, Jacob is old enough to run home and check on Sophie; Jacob is smart enough to make the supper. Does he worry about how much time I spend on my schoolwork when he has chores for me to do?

Jacob filled the dishpan with water and let his darkest thoughts pour into his mind. He thought about the day Mamma died—how long it had taken the midwife to arrive, how Mamma had cried out. *If Papa is such a genius, why didn't he bring home a midwife who knew how to stop her bleeding?*

The dog gave a lazy yawn and curled up in a corner. Jacob felt tired, too. It seemed like these arguments with Papa wore him out faster than lugging pounds of meat up and down the hilly streets. Jacob wished he could curl up in the corner like a dog and never think again. He wished he could wash his mind clean of the last four months and go back to how it was when Mamma was alive, when Papa came home smiling every night. When Papa was proud of his only son.

After the dishes were done, the dog followed Jacob past the chair where Papa sat mending Sophie's socks. As they neared Itzak, the dog padded around in a wide circle to avoid brushing against the man's legs.

CHAPTER 3

DISASTER
BEFORE DAWN

Jacob pulled back the covers and sat on the edge of his bed to take off his shoes. The dog jumped up and curled into a ball at the foot of the bed. Sliding onto his pillow, Jacob poked his feet out of the blanket and let his toes snuggle against the dog's soft fur. Together they drifted into sleep.

The sound of whining woke him. The dog was standing on his bed, tensed as if to run. Propping himself on an elbow, Jacob listened. He thought he could hear another dog barking in the distance. The room was dark and still; his father and sister seemed to be sleeping soundly. Stroking the dog's back, Jacob felt its muscles gradually relax. Finally, it settled down and rested its head on Jacob's thigh. Trying not to disturb it, Jacob eased back onto his pillow.

No sooner had he dozed off than the dog woke him again. This time it was scratching furiously at the covers as though it was digging a hole in a pile of leaves.

"Shhh," Jacob said. He listened, trying to decide if the movement had awakened Sophie or Papa. His sister's even breathing told him that she was still asleep, but he couldn't tell about Papa. Jacob leaned close to the dog and patted its head. "Hush, fella," he whispered.

The dog sat down but kept whining.

"What's going on, Jacob?" Itzak asked in a low voice.

Jacob felt the dog's body begin to tremble.

"Nothing," Jacob said. "He's such a young dog, I guess he misses his mother." Silence. Jacob wished he hadn't said the word "mother." He tapped his thigh softly until the dog nosed his hand. He ran his fingers through the fur around the animal's neck.

Too tense to fall back to sleep, Jacob stared at the shadows on the ceiling. He wished he could think of something to say. Something that would comfort Papa and make him cheerful again. Something that would make their family whole again.

Jacob must have nodded off because he woke with a start. This time the dog was poking him with its damp nose. When Jacob moved, the dog barked. The sound was sharp and loud, like a bullet in the night.

"What's the matter with the doggy, Jacob?" Sophie asked. Her voice echoed against the dark walls.

"Nothing," Jacob began.

"Jacob, that stupid animal has kept me up all night," Itzak said. "I told you there's something wrong with him." Jacob heard the bed creak as his father sat up. "I'm going to put him outside. He's already woken Sophie up. All we need is for the neighbors to complain."

Sophie shot out of bed. "No, Papa! The doggy will get lost. How can he find his way home in the night? He'll be scared."

Jacob stroked the dog's ears while Itzak coaxed Sophie back into bed. "Dogs aren't afraid of the dark," his father told her in a soothing voice, "because they see with their noses. This little dog is probably not used to being shut up inside a closed building so he's nervous. He's used to being outdoors." Itzak patted Sophie's back. Finally she slipped her thumb into her mouth and closed her eyes.

Jacob eased out of bed. "I'll take the dog outside," he

whispered. "I guess I should have walked him after supper." He began to slip on his clothes.

"Be careful, son," Itzak said. "It's almost morning, and wagons will already be on the street. The drivers can't see so well in the dark."

Jacob nodded. "Maybe I'll walk over to the Produce District and wait for Uncle Avi. I'll leave the dog with him." He waited, hoping his father would stop him.

But Itzak did not speak until Jacob opened the door. "It's for the best, son," he said. "You'll see."

Jacob picked up the dog and carried it down the steps. He wasn't sure what time it was, but he heard sounds coming from one or two apartments. Most of the men who lived in their boardinghouse were laborers. Jacob knew that some of them got up before dawn to go to work.

As he opened the outside door, the dog squirmed like a worm on a hook. Then it jumped out of his arms and scrambled onto the street. Jacob could barely keep up as the dog charged down Howard Street. At the corner it began to howl. Jacob squinted, trying to see what the animal was so agitated about. The street-lights were on, but he couldn't see anything unusual. He heard other dogs barking in the distance.

"Is that why you're so restless, fella?" Jacob said. "Because of all the barking?"

The dog cocked its head as Jacob spoke. Then it dropped its chest to the ground, rump in the air, and barked. Leaping up, it ran around Jacob and onto the street. Again Jacob trotted to catch up.

At the next corner, Jacob could hear horses whinnying. *All the animals are skittish,* he thought. *That's strange.* When he reached First Street, Jacob turned north, but the dog darted off in the direction of the waterfront. Jacob slapped his legs, crouched down, and whistled. Finally he coaxed the dog back to his side.

When they reached Market Street, Jacob picked up the dog and carried it in his arms for a few blocks. It was so fidgety—Jacob was afraid it might dash under the wheels of a wagon.

The sky lightened from charcoal to smoky gray, and the streetlights began to dim. As Jacob hurried toward the Produce District, the dog's squirming became frantic. It thrust its hind legs against Jacob's chest and leaped. When it hit the ground, it let out a loud, shrill yelp.

"What's wrong, fella?" Jacob said. "We're going to see Uncle Avi. Come on."

The dog ran a few yards toward the docks, then turned and barked again.

"Not down there, fella," Jacob said. "This way." He trotted up the hill toward the Produce District.

The dog stood, undecided.

Over his shoulder, Jacob coaxed, "Come on, fella. This way."

At last the dog padded to Jacob. Side by side, they ran the rest of the way to Washington Street.

∼

The Produce District was already alive with activity. Jacob saw horses tethered to wooden wagons standing along both sides of the street. Men in overalls were unloading crates and sacks. Jacob breathed in the earthy smells of soil and horseflesh. He passed a wagon heaped high with bulging bags of potatoes and onions. A merchant rushed toward him carrying a stack of egg cartons, and Jacob stepped aside to let the man pass.

As Jacob hurried toward the spot where his Uncle Avi always set up his cart, he started to feel dizzy. His stomach churned, and he thought he was going to be sick. Jacob wondered if Papa was right and the dog had been trembling because of a disease.

The ground started to sway. Bending his knees, Jacob tried to ride the movement. The street heaved and rolled, like the ocean during a storm. It was as though a giant sleeping below the cobblestones had suddenly decided to get up.

Buildings began weaving in and out, and the street pitched like an angry sea. Jacob took a step forward and fell. He heard a wagon overturn and crates thud to the ground. Raising himself on all fours, he tried to make sense of what was happening. *This is an earthquake,* he realized. *It'll be over in a few seconds.* Jacob remembered several earthquakes and how the ground had seemed to roll. Sometimes dishes had fallen off shelves. But in an instant, the quakes had been over.

The street continued to heave and roll. Jacob's ears filled with a roar as loud as thunder. In the gray light he saw the cobblestone street split down the middle. A ditch several feet across opened! As Jacob watched, the ditch yawned wide, thinned to a slit, and gaped apart again.

Bricks were raining all over the street, and the roar was deafening. *I've got to get under something!* Jacob thought. Holding his arms over his head, he rushed toward an open building. He stumbled, then forced himself upright. Something rammed against his legs, and Jacob saw the dog. He could see its mouth moving up and down, but he could not hear it barking. Jacob tried to make his way toward the building again, but the dog tripped him. Frantic, Jacob changed direction and ran toward the other side of the street. A great cracking noise came from behind him. He whirled in time to see the front wall of the building collapse in a heap. The air filled with clouds of dust.

All along the street buildings rattled and lurched. Chunks of masonry hit the ground and broke into pieces. Window glass shattered. The columns on a nearby building buckled and crashed. Carts overturned, littering the sides of the street, and frantic horses struggled to free themselves from their reins.

The dog jumped on Jacob's thigh, pushing him backwards against a collapsed wagon. A pair of horses stampeded through the street toward them. They dragged a broken cart, which lurched from side to side and slammed into piles of fallen bricks. Jacob could feel his heart pounding inside his chest as he squeezed himself against the side of the heavy wagon, hoping it would give him some protection. He reached for the dog and held its trembling body close to his chest. The crazed horses careened by, missing them by just a few feet.

The roaring drowned all other sounds. Crouching beside the wagon, holding tight to the dog, Jacob watched the cobblestones vibrate and buildings cave in. The ground shook with such violence that Jacob thought the world was coming to an end.

The crazed horses careened by, missing them by just a few feet.

CHAPTER 4
AFTERSHOCK

Jacob sat up, startled by the quiet. After the deafening roar of the earthquake, the absence of sound was eerie. The silence around him was so complete, he could hear the pounding of his own heart. Then somewhere far off in the distance, a child began to wail.

Jacob stood up, wiggled his head from side to side, and flexed his arms and fingers. He didn't feel pain anywhere, so he decided that he wasn't injured. The dog looked up at him and wagged its tail, and Jacob bent down to brush the dust off its face and whiskers.

The air had a peculiar, bluish yellow tinge that made everything seem unreal. The Produce District lay in shambles. Piles of dusty rubble littered the street, and some buildings had completely collapsed. Others looked ragged where large chunks of wall had fallen away. Railings dangled off balconies, and the cobblestone street was twisted and pitted. Jacob felt like he'd stumbled into the middle of a nightmare.

Lots of people were on the street. Some fell right to work, righting carts and gathering spilled merchandise. But others wandered aimlessly. Jacob saw one man wearing a nightshirt and walking with a slight limp. He wore a shoe on one foot, but his other foot was bare. A gray-haired woman held a small dog wrapped in a blue shirt. Several people clasped blankets around their shoulders; others carried boxes.

A woman bumped into Jacob. Her hair hung in disarray, and her face was smudged with soot. She carried a baby on one hip, and a small child clutched her skirt. The woman stared straight ahead, but Jacob was sure she hadn't seen him. When she stumbled on a fallen brick, she didn't even look down. Her eyes seemed fixed on something far away.

Nearby Jacob saw two heavyset men pushing with their shoulders against the side of an overturned wagon, while a third tossed aside sacks of onions and pieces of wood. Moans came from under the wagon. At last the workers uncovered an old man wearing an apron. He struggled out, grasping his left arm with his right hand. His shirt sleeve was torn, and blood oozed from a nasty gash on his arm.

Everybody avoided the sides of the street, where debris had fallen in huge piles. Glancing at the buildings, Jacob wondered if any more were going to collapse. He too moved toward the center of the street.

The dog began to bark—a high, excited sound. Jacob followed the dog down the street and saw a horse stuck in a ditch in the street. Only the horse's head and neck were visible. The poor animal's eyes bulged, and a froth of saliva dripped from its mouth. Jacob hurried to help it, but four or five men had already reached its side.

"Would you look at this!" one of them announced. "Poor beast fell right into the crack. Must've gotten crushed. It's dead." The man shook his head in disbelief.

Another man knelt beside the horse and looked into the gap between the cobblestones. The man whistled. "Holy Moses! I guess the street just opened up and swallowed it." The speaker turned to the others and used his hands to demonstrate. "Like a great big jaw—the ground must've opened wide and then clamped shut—squeezin' the life right outta this animal!"

People crowded around to see the wonder, but Jacob backed away. He was beginning to feel sick. So much destruction and horror! He headed down the hill, glancing up frequently to be sure that nothing was going to topple down on him from a damaged building. At street level the air was murky with the dust of collapsed buildings, but above the ruins Jacob could see the morning sun glistening in a clear blue sky. *How can the weather be sunny today?*

Suddenly he felt a jolt. *Another earthquake?* He looked at the people around him. Their eyes were wild with fright. Screams pierced his ears as the ground lurched and began to roll. Jacob fell to his knees and covered his head with his arms. The dog cowered against him.

The aftershock was over in a few seconds, but it energized the street. All at once the dreamy mood of unreality shifted and the entire area came alive with activity. People poured out of buildings carrying children, bundles of clothing, cartons. One man rushed by with a birdcage. All around Jacob people hurried in every direction.

For a second Jacob lost sight of the dog in the crowd. "Here, fella!" he called frantically. When he heard a familiar bark behind him, he whipped around. The dog ran toward him and jumped up. Jacob buried his hands in the thick fur of the dog's neck.

"Where should we go, fella?"

Before the earthquake, Jacob had been heading for Avi's produce stand to return the dog. Now he hesitated. Should he walk back up the hill and search for his uncle? A feeling in the pit of his stomach urged him to keep walking downhill. More than anything else, he wanted to be home with his family. *Papa will be worried sick about me.* Then another thought hit him hard, like a punch. *Papa! What if Papa is hurt? Or Sophie...* Jacob began to run. *Please, God, make them safe.*

Jacob had to slow down to pick his way around the piles of bricks and boards clogging the streets. In places, he scrambled over mounds of debris that completely blocked his way. People stood talking and pointing at the buildings, and Jacob had to squeeze past them. He mumbled, "Pardon me. Excuse me, I need to get through here."

Policemen were blowing their whistles and screaming orders. Horse-drawn wagons clattered down the street, their drivers yelling, "Make way for the horses!" One man glared at Jacob and hollered, "Move over, kid!"

A wagon pulled to a stop in front of a large building. The driver jumped off and hustled up the steps and into an open doorway. Moments later a man emerged and helped a woman in a long dress climb aboard the wagon. Further down the street Jacob saw several men hoisting large trunks onto wagon beds.

On Market Street the cable car tracks jutted out of the ground like mangled springs. Jacob threaded through twisted metal to get across the street.

As he ran, Jacob passed a family pulling a child's wagon piled high with possessions. A little dark-haired girl followed her father, her thumb in her mouth and her face grimy. The girl's eyes met Jacob's. She seemed so small and frightened. A vivid picture of Sophie filled Jacob's mind. He picked up speed and bolted around the family, the dog at his heels.

When they reached the next corner, a policeman blew his whistle to stop them. The road was completely blocked by fallen bricks. Two other policemen were directing eight or nine men as they hauled the bricks off the street. Jacob saw a motorcar idling on the other side of the pile of rubble.

"Clear the way!" the policemen shouted at pedestrians. "We've got to get this car through."

Jacob backtracked and turned onto a side street. He paused to catch his breath. *Where am I?* He knew he'd been heading in the general direction of home, but he hadn't paid attention to landmarks. He decided he'd better stop running willy-nilly because he was beginning to tire. His mouth felt very dry. Hoping to spot something familiar, he scanned the fronts of nearby buildings. He was in one of those streets that always reminded him of a canyon, flanked with tall buildings on both sides. This street had to be part of the business district.

All of a sudden the dog came rushing at him, barking furiously. *Why is the dog running toward me?* Jacob wondered. He didn't even remember the dog leaving his side.

Then he looked beyond the dog, and he felt like he was falling off a cliff. There, only a block away, a full-grown steer was stampeding down the street!

"Look out, sonny!" a voice shouted.

A steer? Jacob stood rooted to the spot. *Why is this happening? Who's yelling?*

A stab of pain snatched Jacob from his stupor. Something was snapping at his fingers and pulling at his clothes. He heard growling and glanced down. The dog was nipping at his fingertips.

The steer was hurtling down the street right at him! Jacob wheeled around, leaped over a fallen chimney, and threw himself against the wall of a building. As if in a dream, he watched the dog scurry out from beneath the pounding hooves of the steer. Dazed, he watched another steer thunder by, then two more.

Jacob heard shots ring out. He looked in the direction of the noise and saw two men with guns chasing after the cattle. One of the men paused and took another shot at the stampeding beasts. A steer keeled over sideways and hit the cobblestones with a thump. Jacob slid down the wall of the building and sat in a heap, his head in his hands.

"You all right, son?" said a voice in Jacob's ear.

Jacob turned his head. A middle-aged man wearing a black overcoat and hat was kneeling beside him. He looked like a well-dressed businessman out for stroll.

"That was something, wasn't it?" The man chuckled, shaking his head. "Never thought I'd see a herd of cattle stampeding through the business district."

Jacob just gawked, too stunned to reply. He felt as if a perfect stranger had strolled right into the middle of his private dream and started a casual conversation.

"Good thing you had that dog with you," the man said. "I kept hollering, but I couldn't get your attention. I believe you would've been a goner if you'd stayed in the street."

Jacob tried to concentrate on the man's words, but they all blurred together in his head.

"Those cattle must've broken loose during the quake," the man continued. "The drivers were probably bringing them over to the stockyards at Portrero before everything went haywire."

Jacob nodded, but he was not at all sure what the man was saying.

The man sat down on a step. "Here, sonny. I took the precaution of filling a jug with water before I left home. Looks like you could use a drink."

When the man held out the jug to Jacob, the dog whined.

Laughing, the man poured a little water into his palm. "Guess you earned a drink, too," he said.

Wagging its tail, the dog approached the man slowly and slurped the water from his hand.

The man patted the dog's head. "That's all I can do for you, pooch," he said. "Don't know when I'll get my hands on any more water." He held out the jug for Jacob.

Jacob took a swig of the water, then another. "Thanks," he said. "I don't know what I was thinking when I saw that steer coming at me. I couldn't move." He handed back the jug.

"Where's your family, son?"

"Don't know," Jacob replied. "I was in the Produce District when the quake hit. I left my father and sister in bed this morning. I was trying to get back home. We live in a house south of Market Street."

"One of those wooden boardinghouses?"

Jacob nodded.

The man frowned. "I saw some folks coming from that direction. They said those houses were in bad shape. Some of them collapsed into a pile of sticks when the quake shook them. They said fires have already started down there. All the gas mains were damaged by the quake, you know."

Jacob gaped at the man.

"Look here, sonny, I wouldn't worry too much. Your family is probably fine. Folks have a way of getting through a calamity," he said. "Especially in this city. Lord knows we've had our share of earthquakes. This morning's temblor sure was something, though, wasn't it?"

Jacob couldn't sit still any longer. Every muscle in his body tingled with fear. He pictured Sophie trapped in the rubble and Papa frantically digging to reach her. He imagined curtains of flame roaring across buildings.

"I appreciate the water, mister," he mumbled as he stood up. "I've got to hurry." He stood up, then grabbed the wall to steady himself.

"You sure you're all right?" asked the man.

Jacob nodded. "I'm fine. Thanks." He stumbled into the street, the dog trotting beside him. Several people were bending over the huge body of the dead steer, but Jacob didn't go back for a closer glance.

When his legs began to feel steady under him, Jacob picked up speed. As he ran, he pictured Sophie's eyes when she was scared—round and dark, like pools brimming with fear.

CHAPTER 5

SOUTH
OF MARKET

B y the time Jacob reached his street, he was panting. The sooty air stung his eyes. With so much dust in the air, he couldn't be sure...but he thought he smelled wood burning.

Pausing to catch his breath, Jacob took a careful look at his neighborhood. The familiar rows of boardinghouses and colorful shops were almost unrecognizable. The sky peeked through gaps where walls once stood. Many buildings had completely collapsed, leaving piles of broken boards between ruined houses. Signs were hanging off storefronts, and merchandise was scattered on the street.

One boardinghouse caught Jacob's attention. Tilting sharply, the structure rested on two of its foundation corners, as if it had frozen in the act of tipping over. A nutty thought popped into Jacob's mind, and he said aloud, "That building looks like it's doing a dance step!" At the sound of his voice, the dog whined and jumped up on Jacob's leg.

"We're almost there, fella. Just a few blocks to go."

Lots of people were on the street and debris was strewn all over the ground, so Jacob had to make his way slowly. Here and there among the piles of boards he spotted a broken chair, a man's hat, a broom handle. The familiar objects reminded him that hundreds of families lived South of Market. He wondered where all those people would go now that their homes were destroyed.

Jacob and the dog passed a man dragging a heavy trunk bound with ropes. The trunk made a rumbling sound as it bumped down the street. Every few minutes its owner stopped, sat down on his trunk, and mopped his forehead with a hand-kerchief.

They ran past an entire family trudging single file down the center of the street, like a row of ducklings. Both parents teetered under a load of blankets, pans, and other household items. Five children followed, from tallest to shortest. The first was a girl with long ringlets who held a violin case and an umbrella looped over her arm. Her four brothers trailed behind her, each carrying a heap of clothes. The smallest child couldn't have been any older than four, but he clutched a bundle of linens as he hurried after his bigger brothers.

Jacob swerved around a young man pushing a baby carriage piled high with towels, books, and a lamp. Walking next to the carriage was a woman who carried a sleeping baby wrapped in a quilt. Several people pushed wheelbarrows filled to overflow-ing with clothes and cooking utensils.

Sightseers also wandered through the streets, stopping to chat and gawk at the damage. A large group of men and women posed for a photograph in front of one of the wrecked buildings.

Just ahead, Jacob noticed four men on top of a mound of rubble. They were straining to hoist massive wooden beams and heave them aside. Two of the men kneeled to look at something, and one cupped his hands over his mouth and began to yell.

Those men are searching for people trapped under there! Jacob realized. His hands felt icy as he forced his legs to move. "Come on, fella, we need to hurry!"

Jacob and the dog had to circle around a crowd of twenty or

thirty spectators who were gathered on the street looking up at a four-story hotel. The front wall of the hotel had simply peeled off, leaving the rest of the building intact. Jacob could see inside every room on every floor. There were lamps sitting on tables, beds with sheets on them, dressers, and shiny mirrors. A painting of a mountain hung against the yellow wallpaper in one room. It was like looking into a life-sized dollhouse.

The cutaway hotel made Jacob remember an afternoon last December. The weather had been mild, so he'd taken Sophie downtown to see the holiday decorations. It was just before Mamma died.

As they gazed in shop windows, Jacob had held his sister's hand. Sophie was fascinated by a fancy dollhouse in one window. He remembered how she had pointed out each miniature object. "Look, Jacob! See the tiny candleholder? It has a real candle in it. And there's a teeny tea set with roses on it!"

Jacob looked down and saw the dog watching him, its head cocked to one side.

"It's all right, fella," Jacob said. "We're gonna find them, you'll see."

When they reached the corner, Jacob had to glance up and down in each direction to be sure he knew where he was. Everything looked so different! The huge Nevada Boarding House had fallen in, leaving a mountain of rubble. Holding his breath, Jacob stared at the space next door. That's when he realized the impossible had happened. *Our house is gone!*

"Nooooo!" Jacob wailed as he charged into the jumble of boards and dust that had been home. "Papa! Are you here? It's me—Jacob! Answer me!"

The dog began barking and people were yelling, but Jacob ignored them. *Where's our apartment?* He had to find his family. He had to find Sophie!

As he scrambled onto the mound of boards, Jacob heard something crack. His foot plunged between some dusty planks, but he was able to break his fall by grabbing onto the corner of a mattress. Pulling his leg free, he continued crawling up the mound. Cautiously he inched across a jagged section of wall and squinted into a cavernlike opening. "Sophie! Papa! Can you hear me?" No voices answered, so Jacob picked his way around the opening and continued searching.

The dog was following him. Barking excitedly, it hopped from board to board. Suddenly it yelped, then began squealing frantically. Jacob looked back, but he couldn't see the animal. He heard claws scrabbling below him, so he kneeled to peer into the darkness beneath the boards. He could see the dog crouching near something that looked like a broken table.

Jacob shoved aside sticks and pipes and lowered himself into the pocket. The debris shifted and caved in around him. He grabbed at a massive headboard to slow his downward slide. Crawling toward the dog, he called, "Here I am, fella, I'm coming."

By stretching out his arm, Jacob could just reach the animal. It was clawing at the rubble with its front paws, but one of its hind legs seemed to be caught under something.

Jacob edged closer. Grasping the dog's body with one hand, he groped around with his other hand until he located its trapped leg. Then he tore away rough pieces of metal and splinters of wood. Carefully he dug around the leg until the dog was finally able to pull it out. As soon as he was free, the terrified animal leapt onto Jacob and knocked him off balance. Jacob barely managed to break his fall by grabbing the edge of a windowsill. He felt a stab of pain in his wrist, but he ignored it.

Clutching the squirming dog as tightly as he could, he edged backwards through the tangle. At last, half crawling, half staggering, he emerged from the pocket. When they were under the open sky again, the dog nestled close to Jacob's chest and licked his chin.

"Hey, kid!" a voice hollered from the street. "Whadda ya think yer doin'? Get offa there before ya break yer neck!"

A man scrambled partway up the mound and held out his arms. Jacob handed him the dog. "My family…" Jacob said hoarsely. "I'm trying to find them. We live in this building."

"Nobody's in this heap, kid. I been crawlin' around these buildings all mornin' lookin' fer folks who might've got trapped. Ain't heard a peep from this one." The man set the dog down near the street and grabbed Jacob's arm to help him scramble off the pile of debris.

"But my family…we live here…" Jacob tried to explain. "They were still in bed when I left…."

"Everybody got outta this house before the walls gave way. Least, everybody who was able to get out."

Jacob studied the man's face.

The man met Jacob's eyes. "Look, kid. There ain't no point in breakin' yer neck tryin' to dig through all this," the man said. "If yer family was trapped in this here building, they're goners, and that's the truth of it. If somebody was still alive here, we would've heard 'em screamin' by now. Lord knows we've heard plenty of screamin' next door, where the Nevada was!"

Jacob hesitated.

"Instead of breakin' yer neck up there, why don'tcha go ask around the street? Maybe somebody's seen yer folks."

Jacob scanned the jumble of boards, railing posts, furniture, and unidentifiable objects that was once their boardinghouse. He really didn't know where to begin tunneling to uncover their apartment, and it was plain that he couldn't sort through this entire mound by himself. The man's suggestion made sense. Maybe somebody on the street had seen Papa and Sophie.

Brushing little nuggets of broken glass off his sleeve, Jacob noticed his wrist was bleeding. But he ignored the trickle of blood and said, "Maybe you know my father? He's pretty tall and thin, with dark hair. Itzak Kaufman's his name. He's a butcher. He would have had a little girl with him—my sister Sophie. She's five. Curly hair and big brown eyes."

The man shrugged. "Sorry, kid. I don't know the name. And yer describin' hundreds of folks down this way."

Jacob nodded, stamping his feet to shake off some of the dust.

The man ripped a length of fabric off the hem of his shirt and motioned for Jacob to hold out his bleeding arm. "I don't see any shards of glass in here," he said as he tied the fabric around the wound. "Better wash it clean when ya get a chance, though."

Jacob sniffed. "Do you smell something burning?" he asked.

The man frowned. "Fire's comin' this way. It's three, maybe four streets over. Fires are startin' all over the city. And with the water lines cracked, ain't no way to put 'em out. Don't know what we're gonna do—" He shook his head. "Even if the city had enough fire engines to go around, how could them wagons get through the mess in the streets? Guess it don't matter down here, though. Who's gonna worry about these cheap boarding-houses, with them big fancy buildings downtown in danger of burnin' up?"

"Hey, Mac!" a voice called from the collapsed Nevada House.

"Over here!" yelled the man who was helping Jacob.

"Think I got somebody. Can you give a hand?"

Jacob followed Mac, who hurried back to the mountain of debris where the Nevada Boarding House once stood.

"Better stay back, kid," said Mac. "Don't want ya gettin' hurt again." He disappeared into what looked like a tunnel leading down into the ground. It was dark at the bottom, and Jacob could see water seeping through the boards. After a few moments Mac and three other men emerged from the hole, balancing the body of a woman on a long board. Jacob helped clear a path for them to the street.

A knot of onlookers crowded around the men, pushing in to see the body as the men laid it down. Jacob looked at their faces and understood that these people were searching for their families, too. When the rescuers carried out a lifeless body, all the people waiting on the street hurried over, praying the dead person wasn't somebody they knew and loved.

Jacob edged into the group. Two of the rescuers were standing with their heads bowed in prayer. Eyes closed, they held their right hands over their hearts. He heard someone wailing. The dog pushed through Jacob's legs and sat on his foot. Jacob bent down and picked him up.

One large man broke away from the group. Mac grabbed the man's arm and said, "Hold on, Callahan. Surely you can spare a minute for a bit of a prayer. This is Duncan O'Connor's mum."

Jacob gasped. *Timothy's grandmother! That's the woman I met last night. I offered to carry her bundles up the stairs for her.*

He stared at the body. Mrs. O'Connor looked so different that he barely recognized her. She was as motionless as a fallen tree, but her eyes were wide open. A long nightshirt clung to her white body, and the skin on her bare legs glistened with moisture. Her gray hair was pasted against her head and her face was puffy. The skin on one side of her forehead was bruised and purple, like something had fallen on her while she was lying in bed.

Forcing himself to shut his eyes, Jacob tried to remember the words of the Kaddish, the Hebrew prayer for the dead that he'd recited so often after his mother's death. But his heart was

Fear washed over Jacob.

thumping so fast that he couldn't think. Icy prickles of terror ran up and down the skin on his arms.

A little girl tugged at the skirt of the woman next to Jacob. "Why is she all wet, Mamma?"

"I dunno. Maybe the water line broke and flooded the bottom floors."

"But where's Timothy? Didn't he live with his granny?" the child asked. "Is Timothy all right?"

"I dunno, child. I haven't seen Timothy, but he might've gotten out earlier. Don't keep pesterin' me with so many questions right now. They been carryin' folks outta there all mornin', and it looks like anybody left in there's been drowned."

Fear washed over Jacob. *What about Papa and Sophie? Please God, don't let them be drowned.*

He backed away from the cluster of people and stumbled into the street, the dog following at his heels. Jacob's stomach was queasy, and his arms and legs felt shaky. He flopped onto the ground and closed his eyes.

The dog nosed Jacob's neck. When Jacob didn't move, the dog whined and licked the boy's nose with its sticky tongue. Jacob sat up and opened his eyes, grimacing at the sour odor of the dog's breath. He stroked the animal's ears while he peered around the street. Lots of people were standing in little clumps on the street, but he didn't see anybody he knew. *I guess most of our neighbors have already left,* he thought. *Where did everybody go?*

Leather shoes were scattered around the street near where he sat. Jacob reached for one. Its heel was missing. *This must be from Mr. Straussberg's shop.* Jacob wondered if the old cobbler, who lived in a room behind his shop, had made it out in time.

Picking himself up, Jacob brushed off the seat of his pants. He took a deep breath and walked over to a man leaning on a wheelbarrow full of clothing. "Pardon me," he said. "My name's Jacob. Jacob Kaufman. We live in that house next door to the Nevada. Have you seen my father—Itzak Kaufman, the butcher? He's got dark hair. He'd have my sister with him. She's only five—dark curly hair."

The man shook his head.

Jacob thanked him and went from person to person, asking the same questions. They all tried to be helpful, but nobody knew Itzak Kaufman. Nobody remembered seeing a man and a girl that matched their description.

"Sorry, son," a tall woman told him. She had tears in her eyes. "I can't find my father, either. He's so crippled up with the rheumatiz that he can hardly walk. I've been searching for him all morning."

"A lot of families got separated," another woman muttered.

"Try not to worry, kid—you'll find 'em."

Finally a freckled woman with a kerchief tied around her hair smiled at Jacob. "I think I know who you're talking about," she said. "Your father's the butcher, isn't he?"

"Yes," Jacob said. He held his breath.

"I used to buy meat from him," she continued. "His wife died not too long ago, right?"

Jacob nodded. "Have you seen him?"

"I saw someone who looked like him on the street this morning. Maybe an hour or two ago. He was carrying a little girl. She had her thumb in her mouth."

"That's her!" Jacob said. "That's Sophie."

They're alive! Both of them. Jacob felt like flying. "Do you know where they went?"

The woman shook her head. "No, can't say I do. But maybe somebody else saw them." She turned and called to a red-haired man in a cap. "Eddie! You remember the butcher, Mr. Kaufman?

He lived in the same building as Fritz. Have you seen him? This is his son."

The man nodded at Jacob. "Kaufman the butcher? Yes, I know your da. Saw him this mornin', I did. Right after the big shake." He looked around the street. "But that was a couple of hours ago. Don't know where he is now. Maybe you got an aunt or granny livin' down here?"

"No, my uncle—" Suddenly a thought flashed through Jacob's mind. "I know where they went! Papa thinks I'm at Uncle Avi's stand. He must've gone looking for me there!" Jacob exclaimed. He shook the man's hand up and down. "Thank you, mister. Thank you." Tears slid down Jacob's cheeks. He wiped them with his sleeves and stammered, "See, I was afraid that…"

"Of course you were!" The man patted Jacob's shoulder. "I understand," he said. "It's only natural. You were afraid your da got crushed when the building fell. That's how any man would feel."

Swallowing hard, Jacob tried to steady his voice. "Well, I'll be seeing you," he said. "Good luck, and thanks again for your help."

Jacob took off at a trot, heading back toward Market Street. The dog bounded along beside him.

CHAPTER 6
RESCUE

Judging by the angle of the sun, Jacob figured that it was past noon when he and the dog got back to the Produce District. He walked up and down the block twice, stopping to ask people if they'd seen his family. But nobody recognized the name Itzak Kaufman or remembered seeing a slim, dark-haired man holding a small girl.

Where are they? He was starting to feel discouraged. *Maybe they didn't come here. Maybe that man got Papa confused with somebody else.*

A policeman was directing traffic on one corner. Approaching him, Jacob said, "Excuse me, officer, I'm looking for my family. My father came up here after the earthquake. He was—"

"Move along, son, and get that dog out of the way! We're tryin' to keep this street clear for emergency vehicles."

Jacob picked up the dog and continued, "But you see, I don't know where they are. I don't know if—" He started to cough. His throat felt as dry as a woolen coat.

The policeman blew his whistle and shouted at a group of people to keep moving.

"Please, sir, I haven't seen my family since the quake."

The policeman glanced at Jacob, his expression softening. "There's a lot of confusion right now, son," he said. "But don't worry, you'll find your family. Have you searched the parks? Lots of folks are over in Union Square."

Jacob shook his head. Union Square was only a few blocks away, but it might as well have been on another continent. He didn't know if he could walk anymore. His legs ached.

Studying Jacob's face, the policeman asked, "Had anything to eat or drink today, son?"

"A man gave me some water."

The policeman stuck his hand into a bulging pocket and brought out an apple. "Here, why don't you eat this? Then have a look-see in Union Square."

Jacob thanked the policeman and took the apple. As he started to go, the policeman called him back. "They're gonna start dynamiting these buildings to keep the fires from spreading. The owner of that grocery store over there has been telling folks to take whatever they can carry out." The policeman pointed to a nearby building. "Why don't you see if there's anything left?"

Jacob hurried over to the little store. He ducked through its doorway and paused to let his eyes adjust to the dim room. Broken glass littered the floor, and the shelves against one wall had toppled over. Jacob took a quick survey of the other shelves, but they had been stripped bare. He checked the floor for fallen merchandise, but all he found was a small sack of spilled flour. When he ran his hand over the surface of a low, dark shelf under the counter, he finally got lucky. He touched something cool and hard. Sliding out a plate covered with a glass dome, he discovered a small wedge of cheese. He peeled off the wax and bit into the cheese, but a whimper at his feet made him pause and look down. The dog whined, tail wagging eagerly. Jacob broke off a piece of cheese and held it out in his palm, and the dog swallowed it in a single gulp.

Just before leaving the store, Jacob spotted a bottle of milk that had rolled behind the door. The glass wasn't cracked, and none of the milk had spilled. He picked up the bottle and sniffed its contents. The milk smelled fresh.

As he left the store, he held up the milk bottle and showed it to the policeman. The man smiled and waved.

Feeling a little better, Jacob headed toward Union Square. As he walked, he kept his eyes open for something he could use as a bowl. Soon he spotted a dented piece of metal. Balancing this makeshift bowl on the ground, he poured some milk into it for the dog. While the dog lapped his share, Jacob held the bottle to his own lips and drank the rest. The cool liquid soothed his throat.

Biting into the apple, Jacob started walking again. He scanned the faces of everybody he passed on the street, but nobody looked familiar. *Papa and Sophie must be in Union Square,* he told himself. *They're probably looking for me.* The apple's juice seemed to sweeten Jacob's thoughts. *Maybe they met up with Uncle Avi and Aunt Rose.*

~

Jacob's route took him along the edge of Chinatown, a section of town that he found fascinating, but also a bit scary. Chinatown's crowded buildings were dingy and rundown, and a distinctive odor lingered about them—a mix of exotic spices, spoiled seafood, and garbage. In these streets, the people dressed differently and often spoke another language. Most of the shop signs were written in Chinese characters. Paper lanterns hung from balconies, and store windows displayed delicate porcelain vases and shoes made of embroidered silk. On street corners, men with skinny braids sold fancy paper fans and little dolls. Papa always warned Jacob that Chinatown was a nest of criminals and told him to avoid the area while he was doing his afternoon deliveries. But Jacob had sometimes ignored his father's warning and cut through this maze of streets and alleyways.

Now, as he skirted this section, the smell of burning wood grew stronger. Waves of heat rose from the closely packed buildings, and billows of gray smoke swirled overhead. Here and there, he could see orange flames licking at the sky. The streets, usually swarming with people, were practically deserted. Suddenly the dog began barking and darted into a narrow side street.

"No, fella!" Jacob shouted. "Come back here!"

The barking continued, shrill and insistent. No matter how many times Jacob called, the dog would not return to his side.

Reluctantly Jacob followed the barking. He found the dog charging at a pile of bricks and broken boards. As he got closer, he could hear a thudding noise coming from under the rubble.

"Anybody down there?" Jacob hollered.

"Help!" a hollow voice answered.

Somebody's trapped! Jacob pulled away a broken gate and cleared a path as best he could. He peered into a dark hole that seemed to be the entrance to a cellar. Something moved in the darkness.

"Help!" a voice called. "Is somebody up there?"

"Yes, I hear you!" Jacob answered. He tugged at a long plank lying across the hole and managed to pull it out of the way. Under the debris he could see some steps. The dog scrambled down.

"Good dog!" the voice said. "You found me. Good dog!"

Peering into the darkness, Jacob could see someone struggling to climb out. The person wore a close-fitting cap, which was covered with fine gray dust, and a collarless coat buttoned up to the neck. A long, skinny braid hung down his back. *A Chinese man,* Jacob thought.

"Are you hurt?" Jacob called.

The man's forehead was shaved up to the band of his cap, which made his head seem as round as an egg and his white eyebrows look like miniature beards. When the man wiped the dust off his face, Jacob was startled. The man's eyebrows were not white at all. They were dark brown, and his face was smooth and unwrinkled. *He's just a boy!* Jacob realized.

"My shoulder hurts, but I think I can move it. Can you give me a hand?"

Jacob reached down and grabbed the boy's arm. Bracing himself, Jacob pulled, and the boy scrambled out of the hole. The boy stamped his feet and slapped his hip-length coat and baggy trousers. A cloud of dust flew into the air and settled onto his cloth shoes.

Grinning at Jacob, he nodded. "A thousand thanks."

"What happened to you?"

"I ran back to get something. We live up there." The boy turned and pointed. His eyes widened. "It's on fire!" he exclaimed. "If I hadn't woken up... if your dog..."

At the mention of the dog, both boys looked at the hole.

Jacob whistled. "Here, fella! Where are you? C'mon, get out of there."

After a few seconds, the dog's head appeared.

"Thatta boy!" Jacob called, but the dog disappeared again. When it reappeared, something dark and damp was in its mouth. Jacob tried to grab the dog, but it backed out of reach. So Jacob sat down and started to lower his legs into the hole.

"You better not go in there," the Chinese boy said. "It could cave in again."

Jacob lay face down over the hole, and the Chinese boy stood behind him, holding onto his hips so he wouldn't fall in. Reaching into the darkness, Jacob grabbed the dog by the scruff of the neck. As soon as he lifted it out of the hole, the dog squirmed free and dropped its prize on the ground.

Jacob took a close look. The lump was furry, with a slender, flesh-colored tail. "That's a dead rat!" Jacob exclaimed.

The Chinese boy grinned. "Plenty of rats in Chinatown," he said. "I think your dog has gotten his dinner."

Jacob laughed. He held out his hand. "My name's Jacob. Jacob Kaufman."

The boy shook Jacob's hand. "I am very happy to meet you. I am San Wei Chang. My father deals in fine porcelain and jades. Our shop is in this building."

Jacob winced. "Is your father...?" He gestured at the collapsed doorway.

"No, Father is in Oakland. On business. He often takes the ferry over. That's where Uncle Huang was taking us after the earthquake."

Jacob looked puzzled.

"My uncle works for my father. He lives in the apartment across from us, above our shop," Chang explained. "My mother can't walk very far, and my brothers are little, so Uncle Huang got the cart to take us to the ferry. But we left in such a hurry! Mother forgot her purse. Uncle was afraid we wouldn't have enough money to pay for the ferry, so I ran back. I was going to cut through this cellar, but I couldn't get the door open. It was jammed. I tugged and kicked at it, then the doorway fell down. I think it knocked me out."

"I got separated from my family, too," Jacob said. "I was in the Produce District when the earthquake hit. I ran home, we live South of Market. Our building was wrecked, and a man said my family had gone to the Produce District. But I couldn't find them there, so I'm on my way to Union Square to look for them."

The roar of the flames was growing louder. Jacob heard a

loud crackling sound, then a dull boom. The boys looked at each other and hurried out of the narrow street.

They waited on the corner, but when the dog didn't follow them, Jacob cupped his hands around his mouth and whistled. The dog came trotting out of the side street, carrying the remains of the rat in his mouth.

"What's your dog's name?" the Chinese boy asked.

Jacob hesitated. He was about to explain that the dog really didn't belong to him. But he thought about how he would have run into a building that had collapsed during the earthquake and how he'd frozen when that steer was stampeding right at him. He made a decision. *I'm not leaving this dog on the street. He saved my life.*

"Quake!" he announced. "My dog's name is Quake."

"In honor of the earthquake?"

Jacob nodded.

San Wei Chang smiled. "I think that's a fine name for a brave animal. If your dog hadn't heard me, I could have died in the fire. He jumped in that dark hole after me."

The boys shook hands before they parted. "I hope you will find your family soon, Jacob Kaufman." The Chinese boy waved and headed down the hill in the direction of the ferry.

Jacob turned west toward Union Square. Quake trotted along beside him.

They hadn't gone more than two blocks when the dog turned and barked. Jacob looked behind him and saw San Wei Chang running to catch up.

"Jacob! Jacob Kaufman! Wait!" he hollered. "I just met my neighbor, Mr. Liang. He said they aren't letting people go down to the ferry. He told me that many Chinese have gone to the parks. Is it all right if I come with you to Union Square? It's possible I will find my mother and uncle there." Embarrassed, he dropped his eyes. "My father says that I should not expect a white person to help a Chinese. But you and your dog saved my life. So I wish to repay you by helping you find your family."

Jacob gave the boy a friendly punch in the arm. "You don't owe me anything. You would have done the same for me, San...um...San Way..."

Chang grinned. "Call me San."

"All right, San," Jacob repeated. "We'll stick together, you and me. And Quake."

CHAPTER 7

UNION SQUARE

Union Square was buzzing. People stood talking in little clusters. Others lounged on blankets, like an audience waiting for an outdoor concert to begin.

The boys stopped at the edge of the square, marveling at the crowd. "I've never seen so many people here," Jacob said.

Ladies in wide hats and long dresses strolled up and down, and Jacob noticed several women pushing baby carriages. Families huddled together, with children perched on top of crates and trunks. A few men sat on kitchen chairs and smoked pipes, and one elderly lady rested daintily on an embroidered loveseat with carved arms. Sewing machines, chairs, paintings, and dressers were scattered about on the grass. A slim man dressed in a top hat and vest leaned against a piano.

"We must search carefully," San said. "I think it would be easy to miss somebody in such a big crowd."

Jacob called Quake to his side, and they began to thread through groups of people. Jacob examined faces, concentrating on the dark-haired men. He heard snatches of conversations in passing. Most of the talk was about the fire. Two men were speculating about which downtown landmarks would stand up to the flames. An old man was telling a story about an earthquake from years ago.

A heavyset man spoke in a loud voice: "If you think we're in bad shape, you should see what's going on in New York! Those folks in the East—they don't know how to handle an earthquake. It's not like here. We've got the finest fire department in the country, and..."

This earthquake struck New York? Jacob had never heard of an earthquake rumbling across the whole continent.

As they walked, Jacob recognized the distinct brogue of Irishmen and the rapid speech of Italians. Many of his neighbors had similar accents, but none of these voices belonged to people he knew.

The two boys reached the other side of the little park and turned back. This time, Jacob changed his strategy. Hoping to spot Aunt Rose, he searched the faces of all the dark-haired women with babies or toddlers. Whenever he spotted a little girl, he paused for a closer look. Oh, how he wished he'd hear Sophie's chatter!

San gestured toward a group of Chinese men sitting near the edge of the park. "Please wait here while I speak with those men," he said.

Jacob sat on the ground. He was sweating, so he unbuttoned his jacket and loosened his collar. The smell of burning wood filled the air, and waves of heat blew into the park from the downtown fires. Columns of gray smoke brushed the sky.

Quake curled up beside him, and Jacob stroked the dog's back. *Papa and Sophie aren't here,* he thought. *I would have spotted them by now.* He wished he could close his eyes and make everything disappear. He was tired of walking and tired of thinking.

Five small boys were rolling a ball with their feet, and Quake perked up his ears. Tail wagging, he took a few steps toward them.

"No, Quake," Jacob said. "Come back here!"

Pausing, the dog let out a small whine then slowly lowered his hindquarters to a sitting position.

Jacob looked up and saw a woman smiling at him. Her blonde hair was combed neatly away from her face, and a golden brooch was pinned on her collar. She wore a long, slim dark skirt and a white blouse with puffy sleeves. At her knees a chubby baby toddled along on shaky legs. The baby reached a pink hand toward Quake and squealed.

"Your dog doesn't nip, does he?" the woman asked.

"Oh no, he's a good dog." Jacob remembered how Quake had behaved around Sophie and added, "He loves little kids."

Kneeling, the woman guided her baby's hand across the dog's fur. "There, there. Doesn't the doggy's fur feel soft?"

The baby strained to touch Quake's tail, which swished back and forth on the ground. "No, no!" the woman said. "Mustn't pull the doggy's tail! Be nice!"

Quake screwed his face into his funny little grin and swabbed the baby's ear with his tongue. The baby began to cry, and the young mother gathered him up. Balancing him on her hip, she smiled at Jacob again. "Is your family out here?" she asked.

"No," Jacob said. "I'm looking for them." He explained how he'd gotten separated from his father and Sophie, then described them to the woman.

"I'm afraid I haven't seen them," she said, shaking her head.

Jacob also described his Uncle Avi's family, but again the woman shook her head.

"So you're all alone?"

"No, my friend's over there." Jacob pointed to the group of Chinese. "With those men."

The woman looked at San with the Chinese men and raised her eyebrows in surprise. She paused, as if making up her mind about something.

"I ought to be getting back now," she said. "My mother-in-law started a little cooking fire over there." She gestured toward an older woman sitting near the steps at the base of the square's tall monument, the Victory Statue. "Why don't you come join us? We'll give you some dinner."

Jacob thanked the woman and watched as she wound her way through the crowd. When he saw San walking back to him, he stood up and brushed off the seat of his pants. Jacob told him about the woman's invitation.

San looked over the crowd in the direction that Jacob was pointing. He seemed uneasy.

"Aren't you hungry?" Jacob asked.

"You go ahead," said San. "I'll wait here."

"But don't you want anything to eat?"

"I think it is better if I stay here."

"I'm sure she meant for both of us to come. I pointed you out when you were talking to those men. She knows we're here together."

Reluctantly San agreed to follow Jacob.

∼

The women were sitting on the bottom step of the statue. Jacob said hello, and the blonde woman looked up and smiled. Beside her, a thin, older woman was turning sausages in a pan over a small fire. As soon as the baby saw Quake, he dropped his bottle and started to crawl toward the dog.

"Have a seat," the blonde woman said, motioning at the ground. She turned to the woman by the fire. "Mother, here are the boys I told you about." Looking at Jacob and San, she said, "Boys, this is my mother-in-law, Mrs. Alexander. And I'm Mary. Mary Alexander."

"I'm Jacob Kaufman," Jacob said, smiling. "And this is my friend, San. San, um...San Wei Chang."

The older woman looked at Jacob and nodded but did not smile. She wore spectacles, and her face was long and narrow. Her gray hair was gathered into a bun under a wide-brimmed hat trimmed with small red flowers. She glanced at San, then turned to her daughter-in-law with a question in her eyes.

"We're all in this together, Mother," the younger woman said. "These boys have gotten separated from their families. We can't let them go hungry."

The older woman pursed her lips, but Jacob barely noticed. The smell of the meat made his mouth water. He stared at the pan on the fire, hardly able to think of anything but the twinge in his belly.

At last Mrs. Alexander removed the pan from the fire and cut the sausages. Then she handed each boy a generous piece on a slice of bread.

Jacob hesitated. At home his family kept the kosher laws. They ate only specially prepared meat—never pork, which Jewish people consider unclean. *I should eat the bread without the sausage,* Jacob thought. He opened his mouth to explain why he didn't want the meat, but the aroma was intoxicating. He was so hungry!

Jacob thought about what Papa had once said. "A Jew should not endanger his life by refusing food," he had said, "even if the food is not kosher." He remembered that Papa had urged Mamma again and again to eat during Yom Kippur last fall, even though it was the highest of the holy days and a day of fasting. Papa said that if she fasted while she was pregnant, it might harm her health.

This may be the only food I'll be able to get, Jacob reasoned. *Surely it would be wrong for me to refuse it.*

Reaching for his portion, Jacob examined it closely. He'd never tasted pork, and he wondered if he'd like it. He closed his eyes and took a small nibble. The taste was good, like the beef he ate at home, but spicier and juicier. Jacob took a bigger bite. He was so hungry that he felt like he could eat for hours and never fill up his empty belly!

Quake let out an eager yip, and Mary started to cut off a hunk of sausage for the dog, too.

Jacob held up his hand to stop her. "No need to give him any, ma'am," he said, his mouth full of food. He swallowed, then explained, "He's already had his dinner." Grinning, Jacob told how Quake had captured a Chinatown rat after they rescued San from the cellar.

Mary chuckled, but her mother-in-law frowned.

"What's your dog's name?" Mary asked.

"Quake," Jacob said.

"Quake? That's an unusual name for a dog," Mary said.

Jacob shrugged. "He was a stray, and he really didn't have any name before today. But after he led me to San trapped in that cellar, the name popped into my head." Jacob stroked the dog's head. "I guess he earned it."

Quake whimpered, a thread of drool dangling from his mouth.

Mary laughed. "I believe he did. So I guess he's earned a little extra dinner, too." She broke off a piece of sausage the size of her thumbnail and tossed it to the dog. Quake gulped the tidbit and padded over to sit in front of her knees.

San ate every crumb of his bread and sausage. Then he wiped his lips with his hand and bowed his head. "A flavorful repast," he said to the older woman. "I offer you my sincere gratitude."

She squinted at San, then looked at her daughter-in-law for guidance.

Mary smiled. "Well, you certainly do speak English beautifully!" she said. "I've never heard a boy use such a grand vocabulary. Where do you go to school?"

"I attend the private school at St. Mary's Church," San said gravely. "You see, my father deals in only the finest porcelain and jades. He says we represent all of China when we greet customers at our shop, so our words should reflect our high standards of quality."

The women glanced at each other again. Jacob could tell they were surprised by San's fancy manner of speaking. For that matter, Jacob was, too. San was the first Chinese boy that Jacob had ever spoken to. Of course, he'd seen lots of Chinese people walking downtown or shopping at his father's meat stand. But they rarely said more than a few mumbled words in his presence.

"My father always says that an education is of supreme importance," San said.

"That's what my father thinks, too," Jacob said. "He says I should thank my lucky stars that I live in America, where every child gets a free education."

"Not every child," San said. "The city schools do not accept Chinese children."

Jacob looked at San. "Really? I didn't know that." Jacob glanced at the two women, but neither of them met his eyes.

San reached over and touched the baby's soft cheek. Without releasing the brown rubber nipple of his bottle, the child responded with a milky smile.

"I think my little Willy likes you," Mary said.

San grinned. "I learned some information that might interest you from the men I was speaking with," he announced.

"Did they have any news about your family?" Jacob asked.

"No, they haven't seen my mother or uncle. But they told me that Chicago has been hit by a tidal wave!" San gestured with his hand to show an enormous wave. His head bobbed up and down for emphasis. "They also said Seattle is under the sea and Salt Lake City has disappeared without a trace!"

Mrs. Alexander shot her daughter-in-law a worried look. "Dear God, Mary! It's just what I was worried about. Remember? Mr. Walsh was just telling us that Los Angeles is burning up. He said this dreadful earthquake was only part of a much larger disaster!"

"Pardon me," San said. "Did you say Los Angeles was damaged?"

She nodded.

"Then all the rest of California is also in trouble?" San asked. His voice was leaden. "Oakland is just across the bay. My father is in Oakland." A single tear rolled down his cheek, leaving a shiny trail across his dusty skin.

Mary put her hand on San's shoulder. "Now look, we don't know if Oakland is in trouble or not. Let's not get ourselves all upset before we know what really happened."

"I heard a man saying that the earthquake hit New York City," Jacob added.

"New York. Chicago. Seattle and Salt Lake City. Who knows where else?" Mrs. Alexander muttered. "Didn't I tell you we should be more careful about using up our food, Mary? If this disaster has hit so many cities, there won't be any relief aid coming in. Won't we be in a pretty pickle? With little Willy to look after, and no food!"

"Mother, please!" Mary sighed. "Remember, Frank told you that we've got to keep calm. These are just rumors. There's no way to get news into the city yet." She looked at the boys. "How could Chicago get swallowed by a tidal wave? That doesn't make a bit of sense—Chicago's nowhere near the ocean! Until we get some real news, it's foolish to believe everything that people are saying."

Jacob picked a blade of glass and twirled it between his fingers. San lowered his eyes as if he'd been scolded.

After an awkward pause, Mary asked San how he'd gotten separated from his family. As he told his story, she nodded sympathetically. While they talked the baby fell asleep on the blanket next to her.

Even though daylight was beginning to fade, the temperature in the park was rising. Lavender plumes of smoke billowed up into the blood-red sky, and the sooty air burned Jacob's nose and throat. The fires made a roaring noise that muffled the sounds of the crowd around them. A light dusting of ash had settled on Mary's skirt and the baby's blanket. It reminded Jacob of the flour that used to collect on his mother's hair and dress when she was baking.

People continued to straggle in and join the crowd in the square. Jacob thought about getting up and searching faces again. But his legs ached, and his full belly made him reluctant to move. If only he could rest a little while longer. He closed his eyes.

A boom startled him.

"What's that?"

"My husband said the army was dynamiting buildings in the surrounding streets," Mary said. "They must be getting close."

"Do you think it's safe to stay here?" Jacob asked.

"I think we're safe enough," Mary said. "Frank says the square is a natural fire break. Flames can't jump across such a wide space between buildings. Anyway, I'm sure the soldiers would make us leave if there was any danger."

The older Mrs. Alexander kept glancing at the street. "What could be keeping Frank?" she asked her daughter-in-law. "He could have walked from here to the house and back again ten times over by now."

"Oh, you know Frank, Mother!" Mary said lightly. "He's probably sharing stories with some of the soldiers. Or he might have offered to help a family carry their trunks and lost track of time."

The older woman kneaded her hands together.

Familiar tunes began to drift over the park. A few people had banjos, violins, and other musical instruments with them. Others chimed in with the melodies. Mary began to sing the lyrics of one song. Her sweet, reedy voice made Jacob think of his mother, of how she used to sing to him and Sophie at night.

Jacob remembered how his father used to tease Mamma about singing off-key. But Jacob didn't care. He'd always loved listening to her voice. Long after he had grown too old to ask for a lullaby himself, he liked to listen when Mamma tucked Sophie into bed with a song.

Another loud boom shook the ground, and conversations all over the square stopped abruptly. Then the piano player banged on his keys as if to echo the dynamite. He struck up a song called "There'll Be a Hot Time in the Old Town Tonight!" People laughed and clapped. A pair of men stood up and danced an impromptu jig.

"Here comes Frank!" Mary announced. She stood, smiling, and held out her arms.

Frank was a tall, athletic-looking man with a neat mustache. He put his arms around Mary and kissed her on the mouth. Then he leaned over and gave his mother a peck on the cheek.

She beamed at him. "Where have you been, son?" she asked. "I was awfully worried about you."

"I got conscripted," Frank said. "A policeman ordered me to help clear the street. He must've nabbed a dozen of us. Insisted we clear all the bricks and rubble off one of them side streets so automobiles could get through. Said all the able-bodied men in the city are expected to help."

The sound of his father's voice woke the baby. Frank picked

up the child and swung him through the air. Willy's squeals made Quake yip like a puppy. Smiling, Frank bounced the baby up and down on his knee until Mary handed him a sausage on a slice of bread.

While her husband ate, Mary introduced him to the boys and told him about the rumors circulating around the park.

"A tidal wave washed away Chicago, eh?" Frank grinned. "Now that's a good one!" He looked at the boys. "Misery loves company, don't it? Here we are—wonderin' if anything's gonna be left of our city after this fire has burned itself out. And people are busy inventin' stories about other cities in worse shape than us!"

"How does it look downtown, Frank?" his mother asked.

"Truthfully, it's pretty bad, Ma. Don't seem like the army can get ahead of them flames," Frank said. "No sooner do the soldiers blow up one building than the wind carries a spark across the rubble and sets the rest of the block on fire. The Grand Opera House has burned up, you know. Even the Palace Hotel is on fire!"

The old woman's forehead creased. She put her hand against her cheek and shook her head.

"What about our house?" Mary asked.

"Sorry, honey, I never could get through. The police have our street blocked off. Wouldn't have done a bit of good if I did get into the place, though. They've given the order to shoot looters, and the soldiers aren't takin' the time to ask questions. It's dangerous to be seen carryin' anything out of a building, even if it really belongs to you."

They sat in silence for a few minutes. Then Mrs. Alexander said she was tired. "I guess we might as well stretch out here and get a little sleep," she said. "It's as good a place as any."

San looked at Jacob. "I see that people are still coming into the square."

Jacob sighed and stood up. "You're right. We should have another look through the crowd." He smiled at Mary. "Thanks again for dinner."

"If you don't find your family here, what will you do?" Mary asked.

Jacob shrugged. "I don't know."

"Why don't you find yourselves a spot to stretch out on until morning?" said Frank.

"It's much too crowded over here," Mrs. Alexander said, gesturing to the area around the statue. "But I'm sure you can find yourselves a little room to sleep." Looking at San, she added, "Maybe over there where you saw those Chinamen."

"Union Square's a safe place to stay tonight, boys," Frank said. "If you don't find your families here, then I'd head for Golden Gate Park tomorrow. I hear lots of folks have gone out there to take shelter."

Before they left, San bowed his head and shoulders. "I will remember your kindness always." Mary and Frank smiled at the boys and wished them good luck.

Mrs. Alexander pursed her lips and said, "I hope you find your people. Both of you."

～

The boys and Quake began to wander through the square again. They wove in and out of groups of people, stopping to describe their families to anyone who would listen. Several other people were doing the same thing. One woman stopped the boys and asked whether they had seen her child, a red-haired boy that she said was a little shorter than Jacob. The woman's voice kept breaking as she spoke. In the glow from the fire, Jacob could see tears shining on the rims of her eyes.

Exhausted, Jacob and San sat down near a clump of bushes.

Against the black sky the flames formed a flickering wall of colors—orange and red darting in and out of the grayish plumes of smoke. It was so bright that Jacob could see San's features almost as clearly as in the daylight.

"You said your mother can't walk very far?" he asked San.

"Her feet are bound."

"Bound?" Jacob asked.

"So they will remain small. It's an old Chinese custom. The mark of an upper-class woman." San was quiet for a minute, then he turned to Jacob. "And your mother? You have not mentioned her. Only your father and your sister, Sophie."

"My mother died," Jacob said, "last December. She was having a baby."

"And the baby?"

Jacob shook his head. "Dead, too. It was a boy. It would have been my little brother."

"I am deeply sorry," San said.

After that, the boys stopped talking. They lay down on their backs beside each other, and Quake crawled in between them. As the two boys stroked the dog's fur, Quake stretched out his front paws, rested his head on Jacob's chest, and shut his eyes.

Jacob watched the flames for what seemed like hours. In his thoughts, he retraced his day, from before dawn when he first left home until afternoon, when he arrived in Union Square. He kept telling himself that Papa and Sophie were all right. But questions kept flashing into his mind. *Why didn't I find them in the Produce District? Where are they? Where should I go looking for them tomorrow?*

A fine dusting of ash sifted onto Jacob's clothes, his hair, and everything he touched. The smoke and ash were stinging his eyes, and he squeezed his eyelids shut. But he knew it wasn't just smoke that caused a drop of water to roll down his cheek and pool in his ear. He was scared, as scared as he'd ever been. Although Union Square was jammed with refugees, Jacob felt alone and stranded, like the only survivor of a shipwreck.

When he finally began to doze, he dreamed he was a little boy and it was a sweltering summer night in their boardinghouse. Mamma sat in a kitchen chair by the open window. He padded out of bed and pushed another chair close to hers. Then he curled himself onto his chair and laid his head on Mamma's lap. Her bony knees made a hard pillow, but he refused to crawl back into his own bed.

Mamma began to sing, her voice sweet and reedy, her soft hand resting on his chest. Smiling proudly, Papa watched over them.

CHAPTER 8
SWEET AND SOUR

Jacob woke to a hand gently shaking his shoulder. Although his nose was stuffy from the smoky air, he smelled something delicious. He opened his eyes and saw San kneeling beside him, smiling. On the ground were three small round bowls filled with steaming noodles.

"I brought breakfast," San said, "for us and for Quake."

Quake was already nosing the bowls and gingerly licking at the hot food.

"Better eat yours fast," San said as he picked up one of the bowls. "Before Quake saves you the trouble."

Quake took a few quick nips at a bowl of steaming noodles. As soon as the food began to cool, the dog gulped it down. He lapped the broth in the bottom of the bowl, swabbed it clean with his tongue, then sat in front of the boys and whined.

Jacob propped himself on an elbow and reached for a bowl. He didn't see a spoon, so he snatched up a noodle with his fingers and sucked it into his mouth. It was a little salty, but he liked the savory flavor.

"Here, I brought chopsticks for you." San held out two smooth sticks.

Jacob took them and watched as San held both chopsticks in one hand and used them to lift noodles and slide them into his mouth. Jacob tried to copy San's movements, but his noodles slipped off the sticks. Impatient, he picked up the bowl and took a big slurp. Jacob tasted bits of crunchy vegetables and chewy lumps of meat mixed with the noodles. Broth dribbled down his chin, and he wiped it off with his hand as he leaned forward for another bite.

San put his bowl in his lap and leaned forward to position Jacob's fingers around the chopsticks. It took a little practice, but Jacob finally managed to control the sticks.

"Where'd you get this?" Jacob asked.

"From the men I saw yesterday." San finished his noodles, tilted his bowl to his lips, and drank the broth. Jacob imitated his friend, then ran a finger around the inside of his bowl and licked it clean.

"I'll take the dishes back," San said, gathering the empty bowls and chopsticks.

Jacob got up stiffly and brushed himself off. "I'll come with you. Then we can head for Golden Gate Park."

On one side of Union Square a group of about twenty Chinese men and women sat on the ground around a makeshift stove they had built with a ring of stones. A black lidded pot rested on the stones.

"Thank you," San said and handed the dishes to a tiny brown woman stooped over the pot.

Jacob faced the woman and bowed his head and shoulders as he'd seen San do yesterday. "A flavorful repast," he said, echoing his friend's words. "I offer you my sincere gratitude."

The woman looked at Jacob as if he was a strange insect. She didn't nod or speak.

Jacob scanned the rest of the group for a reaction, but the men avoided his eyes.

San began to speak to the men in Chinese. The words sounded short and punchy to Jacob, who couldn't understand anything that was said. As the boys turned to go, the men raised their hands and waved.

"What did you tell them?" Jacob asked.

"That we're going to Golden Gate Park. So if they see my mother or uncle, they can tell them where I am."

"Does that woman understand English?" Jacob asked as they skirted the edge of the square. "I just wanted to thank her for the noodles."

San grinned. "She understands some English. But she works in a laundry. She is not used to such fancy language. It made her uncomfortable."

Jacob's cheeks turned red.

"No matter," said San cheerfully. "I'm sure she thinks white people are odd anyway."

~

The boys left the square and set off through the smoky streets, Quake trotting along beside them. Sometimes they had to backtrack or detour because firefighters and soldiers had barricaded entire blocks. Twice they had to stop and ask directions. But mostly they kept the plumes of smoke above the downtown buildings at their backs. Catching glimpses of blue sky over the Pacific Ocean, they headed west.

The sun was high in the sky by the time their roundabout route brought them to Polk Street. Jacob stopped to take off his jacket and roll up his sleeves. It was a warm day, and the smoke and fires were making him sweat.

A group of soldiers were gathered around a horse-drawn wagon parked in front of the buildings on the eastern side of Polk. Nine or ten boys around Jacob's age were standing on the other side of the street, near the corner of Sutter. Pointing at them, Jacob said to San, "Let's go see what they're doing." He started across the street.

San hesitated, then hurried to catch up with Jacob.

Three of the bigger boys were talking to a short man in a

dirty white shirt. The man listened, then nodded and grinned. Immediately the boys burst into smiles and sprinted toward an open doorway. The others began cheering and rushed across the street to join their friends

"C'mon!" Jacob called as he ran toward the boys. Quake darted after him. San followed reluctantly.

When they came in sight of the doorway, Jacob read the sign: Blum's Candy Store. He turned and called to San. "It's a candy store! Hurry!"

Jacob ran inside. Boys were scooping handfuls of candy out of the barrels and grabbing boxes off the shelves. He asked what was going on.

"They're gonna blow up all the buildings on this block," a boy said. "That man told us to take whatever we can carry!"

Jacob went back to the doorway. San was in the middle of the street, crouched on one knee, with his arm around Quake. Jacob motioned for him to come in, but San shook his head. Jacob shrugged. He assumed San was trying to keep the dog out of the store.

Inside, the boys laughed and talked while they stripped the shelves. They began to stack boxes by the entrance. "We're gonna go find something to put all this in!" one shouted as five or six of them ran outside.

Jacob stuffed some all-day suckers in his pocket, then tucked boxes of jelly beans and marshmallows under his arm. He turned to leave, but stopped when he remembered Sophie and Avi's twins. He grabbed three more suckers and balanced a box of chocolate chips on top of his pile.

He heard a commotion outside. Jacob looked out the window. Quake was barking and lunging at a boy's legs. The boy was yelling, and another boy picked up a brick and threw it at Quake.

"Quake, c'mere!" Jacob hollered, running out of the store. "Hey, you! Don't hurt that dog!"

The boys turned. That's when Jacob realized that that one boy was holding San by his pigtail. San's eyes were squeezed shut and his face was twisted in pain. Another boy was jabbing a sucker stick at San's face.

"Chinaman likee candy?" the boy with the sucker taunted. "Show us how Chinaman eats with sticks!"

"Stop! Let go of him!" Jacob screamed. He dropped his boxes and hurled himself at the boy holding San's hair.

The boy was much taller than Jacob. He reached out with his free hand and grabbed Jacob's collar. Jacob struck at the boy's face, but his arms weren't long enough. Twisting out of the bully's grasp, Jacob rammed his head into the larger boy's chest. The boy grunted and released San's pigtail as he charged at Jacob.

The rest was a blur. Quake growled, leaped, and clamped his teeth onto the big boy's arm. The boy screamed and tried to shake the dog off, but Quake held on. San kicked the bully's shin. Jacob saw the dog let go of the boy's arm and scramble through San's legs. The next thing he knew, Jacob was being whisked away by the sleeve.

San had pulled him halfway down the block before Jacob remembered the boxes of candy. "Wait!" he shouted. "I left my candy back there!"

San raised his eyebrows and looked at Jacob. "If you go back there, that boy will knock your teeth out. How will you eat the candy?"

Jacob laughed. "I guess you're right!"

They slipped between two buildings to catch their breath. Panting, Quake sat down in front of them. "I wish we had something to drink," Jacob said. Remembering the suckers in his pocket, he pulled them out and offered one to San.

San's eyes were squeezed shut and his face was twisted in pain.

San took the sucker and leaned against the building. Jacob peered around the corner. "Look at that," he whispered. Several boys had pushed a cable car caboose to the front of the store. The others were loading it with dozens of boxes of candy.

"There was more than enough candy for all of us," Jacob said as he licked his sucker. "All you were doing was keeping Quake from running in the store. I don't understand why they started beating you up."

San said nothing. He twirled the sucker stick between his fingers.

"Has that ever happened to you before?" Jacob asked.

"I hate this stupid pigtail," San muttered.

"Why? Most Chinese men wear them, don't they?" Jacob asked.

San frowned. "Yes, to show our loyalty to the Manchu dynasty—the Horse dynasty," San said. "The royal family of China."

"So why do you hate it?"

"That's what they always grab," San said. "When they come looking for trouble, they grab my pigtail. So I cannot run away."

"You should have yelled for help," Jacob said. "There were lots of policemen and soldiers down there."

San looked at Jacob. "You can ask a policeman or soldier for help. I am Chinese, remember?"

"That doesn't matter. A policeman wouldn't have let those boys beat you up."

"No? There was a policeman standing at the corner talking to a bunch of soldiers when the boys came out of the store," San said. "He was looking right at me when that boy grabbed my pigtail."

Jacob didn't know what to say. He gnawed on the edge of his sucker.

After an awkward silence, Jacob said, "I took more suckers. For Sophie and my cousins. I should have taken some for your little brothers, too. But you can have these, if you want." Jacob pulled the extras out of his pocket.

"Thank you, Jacob Kaufman," San said, but he didn't take the candy. "You fought that bully. He was strong, and you were very brave."

"He was pretty big, wasn't he?" Grinning, Jacob punched San's arm. "You didn't do so bad yourself!"

San looked away.

They stayed in the shadow of the building and watched the boys push the candy-filled caboose down the street. As soon as the cable car was out of sight, several soldiers ran into the candy store carrying crates. Other soldiers ran into the buildings beside the store.

After a few minutes, two soldiers jumped into the wagon and drove it down the street. The others came out of the last building on the block and headed up a cross street. A policeman shouted for everyone to clear the area.

"Guess we better get moving," Jacob said. "Do you think we'll make it to Golden Gate Park before dark?"

"I don't know," San said. He was still avoiding Jacob's eyes. "I've never walked that far. I think it is many miles from here."

"You're not sore with me, are you?" Jacob said. "I didn't know those boys would treat you like that. I just thought it was a chance to get some candy."

San turned and started walking.

"Look, we don't have to stay together," Jacob said, "if you don't want to."

San looked at Jacob. "I guess I am sore, as you say. Not with you—it was not your fault, Jacob Kaufman. I am sore because people think they can bully us. Sore at my father, for making me wear this stupid pigtail. I am just plain sore—that's all!" San kicked a brick. His cloth shoe offered little protection, and he winced at the pain in his toe.

Quake trotted over to San and nosed his foot.

Bending over, San stroked the dog's ears and neck. "You also fought those boys for me, Quake. A thousand thanks for your bravery. I think you are very honorable, and so is your owner. You are my friends. You are friends of the Chinese people."

Jacob put his hand on San's shoulder. "C'mon. When we get to Golden Gate Park, I'll introduce you to my father. He'd never be mean to you just because you're Chinese."

As soon as he said it, Jacob wondered if it was true. The only time he'd ever seen Papa speak with Chinese people was when he was selling meat to them.

Now that Jacob thought about it, he realized that all of the Kaufmans' friends were Jews who had moved to America from Poland, just like Jacob's family. Everybody else was a "stranger," and Papa had always warned Jacob and Sophie to be careful around them. Whenever Jacob did something that Papa didn't like, Papa asked him, "Is that the way a Jewish boy should behave?"

San certainly isn't a Jewish boy, Jacob thought. Maybe Papa wouldn't approve of his son hanging around with a Chinese boy.

Another uncomfortable thought popped into Jacob's mind— he'd ignored the kosher laws when he'd eaten the Alexanders' sausage and the soup from that Chinese woman in Union Square. Squeezing his eyes shut, Jacob promised God that he'd obey the kosher laws again, just as soon as this disaster was over. *If only I can find Sophie and Papa,* Jacob vowed silently, *I'll never disobey again.*

Then he remembered that his father had told him to get rid of the dog.

Quake saved my life, he thought. *It wouldn't be right to abandon him now. And San is my friend, what does it matter if he's Chinese?*

Jacob tried to push these thoughts out of his mind. But an even more disturbing thought kept tugging at him: *What if Papa and Sophie aren't in Golden Gate Park?*

CHAPTER 9
SAN FRANCISCO
IN RUINS

When they reached Van Ness, the two boys stopped, astounded by the size of the houses on both sides of the avenue. Jacob had never seen such magnificent homes. Most of them stood solidly on their own ground—not like the squeezed-together apartment buildings downtown. Even the street seemed grand and expensive—it was wider than any of streets in Jacob's neighborhood or downtown.

Each house was as large as a hotel and painted a deep, rich color. As he passed by them, Jacob tried to peer through their shiny windows, beyond the fringed shades and thick drapes, hoping for a glance at the things that such wealthy people would own. But all he could see in the glass panes were reflections of the plumes of smoke from the downtown fires.

The walls of the mansions curved in and out, like the scalloped edges of an afghan. Delicate strips of carved wood adorned the roofs, and the balconies were decorated with pretty little fences. Jacob ran his fingers along a wrought iron railing that separated one of the houses from the street. A curlicued vine of metal leaves ran along the top of the gate.

The boys spotted a tiny Chinese woman sweeping the front steps of one enormous house. "Hello," San called out.

The woman looked up and smiled.

"Do you have water?" San called. "We are thirsty."

Nodding, the woman held up her index finger and said, "You wait." She darted inside the house.

She returned quickly, holding two large glasses of water. "Come, you sit," she said in choppy English and gestured toward the porch steps. "Drink."

Thanking her, the boys took the glasses and sat on the steps. Jacob was so thirsty, he gulped the entire glassful without stopping for a breath. When he lowered the glass, he noticed that Quake had sidled up to the Chinese woman and was nosing her hand.

"Ah, nice dog," she said. "Maybe thirsty, too?" Again she hurried into the house. Returning with a bowl, she set it on the lowest step. Quake stuck his nose in the bowl and slurped noisily.

"Walking far?" the woman asked as the boys handed her their empty glasses.

"From Union Square," San answered. "We are on our way to Golden Gate Park."

"Ah. Many peoples walk this way. To Western Addition. Golden Gate Park. Fort Mason." The woman grinned. "Very long walking. So tired. Put down heavy trunks." She pointed to five or six trunks that had been abandoned on the opposite side of the avenue.

Jacob raised his eyebrows. "Aren't the owners worried that somebody will steal their stuff? Or that it'll get burned up in the fire?"

The woman shrugged. "Maybe fire cannot come here. Very wide street," she said, spreading her arms apart to demonstrate. Looking at San, she added, "Not like Chinatown."

"Is this your house?" Jacob asked her. Around the entranceway, thick white columns held up a semicircular balcony. The door was a rich mahogany color.

"Not my house!" The woman giggled. "Only kitchen mine."
Jacob looked puzzled.

"Belong Mr. Edwards," the woman explained. "I am cook.
But no cooking today. Maybe gas leaking—spark start more
fire. So, cooking outside today." She grinned. "After big earthquake, have picnic!"

The boys described their families and asked if the woman had
seen them.

Shaking her head, she said, "Many peoples coming.
Yesterday. All this day. But maybe not your families, I think."
She paused, then added, "Many peoples stay at Mr. Merrill's
house. Maybe you go there?" She pointed down the street. "At
corner, Washington Street. Very kind, Mrs. Merrill. Husband,
Mr. Merrill, head of Red Cross Society. Maybe one hundreds
peoples stay that house."

Jacob and San turned to each other. "Let's try it," Jacob said.
"If our families started walking this way, they could have
stopped there. You said your uncle would have to push your
mother and brothers in a cart. And my father would have to
carry Sophie—I know she couldn't walk this far by herself.
Maybe they heard that the Merrills are taking people in."

Thanking the woman again, the boys called Quake and
headed down Van Ness Avenue.

◦∽

Jacob and San had no trouble finding the Merrill Mansion.
Dozens of men and women were sitting on the front steps.
Although some were fashionably dressed, most of them looked
like ordinary laborers. A few children played on the sidewalk.

Approaching an older man, the boys learned that Mrs.
Merrill had welcomed refugees into her home after the earthquake, and many of them had spent the night. All kinds of

refugees were staying there—Irish, Italian, Jewish, Chinese. "The only thing she asks," he said, "is that everybody be as quiet as possible because she's caring for an ailing relative upstairs. Go ahead, just let yourself in the front door," he urged. "But I think you better leave the dog outside."

"I'll stay out here with Quake," San volunteered. "You go inside first."

Jacob walked up the steps and opened the front door. For a full minute he stared at the sitting room. Every inch of it glittered and gleamed! Lamps with round glass shades sat on glossy tables. Two armchairs and a sofa were covered with deep green fabric. A jewel-toned carpet with fringed edges rested on the polished floor, and large portraits in heavy gold frames hung on the papered wall. This was how Jacob imagined a palace would look. He could hardly believe that he was allowed inside.

Easing into the room, he ran his hand across the cool surface of a marble-topped table and fingered the beads hanging from a lampshade. Then he glanced nervously at the people sitting in the room, expecting to be scolded for touching such expensive objects. But nobody seemed to mind. A woman in a long dark dress smiled at him and held a finger to her lips. She gestured with her head at an old man sleeping on one of the chairs. The man had long white sideburns, and his head drooped forward onto his chest.

Nodding, Jacob tiptoed into the next room and approached a group of men. He introduced himself and described his father and Sophie, as well as Uncle Avi's family. The men listened politely, but none of them remembered seeing Jacob's family.

Going from room to room, Jacob repeated this conversation at least twenty times. No one knew his father or uncle or recalled seeing people who fit their description. There must have been sixty refugees in the house. Jacob didn't find anybody that he recognized, but he did meet two families who lived south of Market Street.

He returned to the entranceway, passing the old man who was still asleep on the armchair. The woman in the dark dress smiled, but Jacob didn't return her smile. He was getting discouraged. *Thousands and thousands of people live in San Francisco,* he kept telling himself. *Everybody's leaving because of the fire. I'll find Sophie and Papa, I've just got to keep looking.* He let himself out the front door.

As soon as he saw San, Jacob knew his friend hadn't found his mother on the grounds out back. "Your turn to look inside," he said.

San nodded and made his way up the steps.

Jacob bent over to pet Quake. "C'mon, fella, let's see if we can spot someone we know out here." Again Jacob went from group to group describing Papa and Sophie, Uncle Avi and Aunt Rose to every person on the Merrill grounds, but nobody remembered seeing them.

After circling the house, Jacob sat down on the front steps. Near him, several men huddled around a heavyset fellow who was reading aloud. One man had his back to Jacob. Something about the way the man stood—straight, with his head tilted slightly to one side—reminded Jacob of his father. The man was the same height as Itzak Kaufman, and his black hair was also edged with gray.

"Papa?" Jacob whispered. He jumped to his feet, hardly daring to hope. His heart hammered in his chest. Edging around the group, he finally got a clear view of the man's face. In an instant, Jacob's excitement evaporated. The man had a mustache and his skin was like leather. Jacob swallowed hard to get rid of the lump that had filled his throat, but the men weren't paying any attention to him. They were concentrating on the heavyset fellow who was holding an open newspaper.

Suddenly Jacob realized the importance of what he was seeing: *A newspaper! He has a newspaper!* Across the top of the page Jacob saw the names of all three of San Francisco's newspapers: *The Call–Chronicle–Examiner.* He squinted at the date across the top: Thursday, April 19, 1906. *That's today.*

The big headline on the front-page story read: **EARTH-QUAKE AND FIRE—SAN FRANCISCO IN RUINS.** Jacob strained to read the words underneath the headline: "Death and destruction have been the fate of San Francisco. Shaken by a temblor at 5:13 o'clock yesterday morning, the shock lasting 48 seconds and scourged by flames that raged diametrically in all directions, the city is a mass of smouldering ruins."

Jacob skipped to the second paragraph. "After darkness, thousands of the homeless were making their way with their blankets and scant provisions to Golden Gate Park…"

As he scanned the rest of the article, one sentence caught his eye. "The number of dead is not known but it is estimated that at least 500 met their death in the horror." He felt a prickly sensation run up his back.

Jacob's eyes darted to the headlines along the bottom:

NO HOPE LEFT FOR SAFETY OF ANY BUILDINGS
BLOW BUILDINGS UP TO CHECK FLAMES
WHOLE CITY IS ABLAZE

The fellow holding the newspaper stopped reading and looked up. "At least we can expect some help from Oakland," he said. "If the reporters from all three papers could get across the bay to print this joint edition and bring it back here to San Francisco, then folks ought to be able to get food and medicine over here, too."

"I thought Oakland got hit," another man said.

"Not according to this paper. And that tale about New York City—that's a lot of malarkey! Nothing in here about disasters in other big cities."

"Now there's a relief!" said the leathery man with the mustache. "I heard Mrs. Merrill saying that boatloads of food and blankets will be arriving from other cities as soon as the news gets out."

"Thank God we live in America!" one of them said. "When the chips are down, folks'll help each other out."

Jacob heard Quake bark. The dog stood by the front door wagging his tail, and San was bending over to scratch the animal's chin.

Jacob joined them. "Any luck?" he asked.

San shook his head. "I found a merchant I know from Chinatown, but he hasn't seen my mother or uncle. He advises us to stay here instead of going to Golden Gate Park. He says we will be better off here because the Merrills will be sure to get food and water from the Red Cross."

Jacob interrupted to tell San about the newspaper.

"So Oakland is safe!" San let out a long breath. "If Uncle Huang found a boat to take Mother and my brothers across the bay, they have all reached my father by now. I think they are safe." San smiled at Jacob. "Today is a lucky day, Jacob Kaufman. Soon we will learn some good news about your family."

The boys began to discuss whether it would be better to remain at the Merrill house or continue walking to Golden Gate Park.

As they talked, a man came panting up the street. "I need to speak with Mrs. Merrill. It's urgent!" the man announced breathlessly.

A hush fell over the people on the steps as someone went into the house to find Mrs. Merrill. In a few minutes she came to the front door and greeted the messenger. She spoke in a composed voice. "I'm told you need to speak with me."

"Yes, ma'am. I have orders to tell you that everybody must leave this house. We're going to destroy it in half an hour! We've got to make sure the fire doesn't spread across Van Ness."

Jacob stared at the messenger. *Destroy this house?* He thought about the splendid paintings he'd seen, the polished wood and chandeliers.

Mrs. Merrill calmly thanked the messenger, but Jacob noticed how the color drained out of her face. She whispered, "My beautiful home!"

Pausing to catch her breath, Mrs. Merrill looked at the refugees on the steps and said, "I do not want anybody to leave until you have all had some tea and toast."

As soon as she went inside, everybody started buzzing.

"You know it's bad if they're gonna blow up this house!"

"I don't know why they need to destroy this place. Even if the houses on this side of the street do catch fire, how can the flames jump across Van Ness? Look how wide this avenue is!"

"If you ask me, I'd rather see the army blow up a few fancy houses than wait for them to catch fire and send sparks across Van Ness. You don't want the flames spreading all the way to Golden Gate Park, do you?"

People began streaming out the door. Someone said servants were packing the family's valuables in a fireproof safe.

In a few minutes, two servants came outside carrying a large silver tray. Setting the tray down, they began serving tea and buttered toast to the refugees.

When Jacob got to the front of the line, the serving girl handed him an extra slice of bread. She nodded at Quake. "So your dog has something to eat, too."

Jacob thanked her and ate his toast quickly. The two boys gulped down their tea and joined the people pouring across the street.

The crowd gathered on the western side of Van Ness. Silently Jacob and San watched the servants hurry out the Merrill's front door. The last to leave the house was Mrs. Merrill, her arms supporting a frail older woman wrapped in a shawl.

As soldiers swarmed up the steps of the mansion, more people gathered to watch. The boys had to stand on tiptoe to see between the other onlookers. Jacob heard a crash and peeked around a man's shoulder. The house's windowpanes had been broken, and jagged pieces of glass jutted from the painted window frames.

After several minutes, soldiers came running out of the house and sprinted across the street toward the crowd. Quake barked. Jacob picked him up and held him against his chest.

Soon a muffled bang rocked the street. With a heartbreaking crack, the walls of the beautiful mansion buckled. Jacob got a split-second glimpse of the walls dropping before a mushroom-shaped cloud of gray-brown smoke rose from the ground. The cloud puffed out and enveloped the house, and a great thudding boom announced that the walls had hit the ground. The crowd gasped.

Jacob thought of the glass lamps and marble tables, the paintings and rugs and sofas. The Merrill mansion, the most beautiful house he'd ever seen, was now just another heap of rubble.

The cloud of smoke hung in the sky as the crowd began to disperse. The boys fell into step with the others, heading west toward Golden Gate Park. They walked silently, absorbed in their own thoughts. In his mind, Jacob kept seeing the walls of the mansion buckle and fall.

CHAPTER 10
GOLDEN GATE PARK

After the dust and smoke of the city, Golden Gate Park looked cool and inviting, like an oasis in the desert. Jacob had expected this park to be larger than Union Square, but he was surprised by how immense it was. The lush green swath extended to the west as far as he could see.

The afternoon sun had faded by the time the boys finally reached the entrance to the park, and the evening air smelled cool and earthy. An aroma of cooking food mingled with the fresh scent of soil and leaves.

Everywhere Jacob turned he saw groups of people in makeshift camps. Some of them had strung blankets between trees to serve as tents. Women hovered over campfires and stirred cooking pots. Some men read or smoked; others lounged on trunks or strolled through the greenery. One woman sat on a park bench and bounced a baby on her knees while two small children skipped around her. An old man with a stiff gray beard was sleeping on a blanket that had been suspended like a hammock between two trees.

"So many people!" San said. "I am sure we will find your family here, Jacob."

The boys followed a path into the park. A squirrel scampered by and Quake chased it up a tree. In a campsite on the other side of a clearing a little black dog began to bark. It ran across a mound of green earth and charged at Quake, the tufts of fur on its shoulders standing straight up. Circling each other, both dogs sniffed cautiously. When the black dog lunged, Quake squealed and scooted away, tail tucked between his legs. Both Jacob and San smiled.

Noticing a policeman on the path, Jacob jogged to catch up to him. "Excuse me, sir. I've lost my family. I came here hoping—"

"There's a tent set up for orphan children, sonny. I'd take you over there myself, but I don't have the time just now. You're a big boy, though, you can't miss it." The policeman pointed. "Just keep on this path, then turn—"

Jacob shook his head and tried to explain. "No, that's not what I meant. I'm not an orphan, I just don't know where my family is. You see, I was downtown when the earthquake struck, but they were home. Our house got destroyed, and when I went back to find them, they..."

The policeman put his hand on Jacob's shoulder and leaned over to look him in the eye. "I understand, sonny. Lots of families got separated one way or another. But you'll be fine, don't you worry. The folks in the children's tent will look after you. I'm sure your mother will come and get you as soon as she can."

Jacob started to say that his mother had died months ago, then stopped. *It's no use,* he thought. *There are probably dozens of kids wandering around, looking for their families.* He turned back and rejoined San.

"They've got a tent for orphan children," Jacob said. "But let's look around first, maybe we'll spot someone we know."

The boys began to introduce themselves and tell their stories to the people camping nearby. Each time Jacob described his family, an image flashed into his mind of the rubble where their boardinghouse had been. He imagined Sophie screaming and struggling under the pile of broken walls and furniture. He remembered the wet body of Mrs. O'Connor stretched on a board, and he pictured his father bruised and lifeless, like her. *I should have kept searching,* he thought. *What if they were under all that broken stuff? Maybe they were trapped, and then the fire came…*

As it grew darker, Jacob started to get discouraged. Nobody knew Itzak Kaufman or had seen a man and girl who matched Jacob's description of his family. *It's like they've disappeared,* he thought. The park's peaceful setting only made him feel more desperate. He picked up a pinecone and heaved it into the trunk of a tree.

Quake chased the pinecone, then flopped down beside the path and rested his head on his paws.

San rubbed his eyes. "I think we should look for someplace to sleep, Jacob. Even Quake is worn out."

Jacob frowned.

"Tomorrow we will have strength again," San said. He put a hand on Jacob's shoulder. "Then we will continue our search."

Jacob shrugged off San's hand and kicked a pebble off the path. "All right," he sighed. "So now we go to the tent for orphans." The word tasted dry and bitter in his mouth.

⁓

A soldier stood guard at the entrance to the orphans' tent. Jacob walked up to him and explained how he'd gotten separated from his family. The soldier listened, nodded drowsily, and motioned Jacob in. But when San started to follow, the man lowered his rifle to block the way.

"This here tent's for lost or orphaned American children," the soldier said. "No Chinese. Most of your kind went to the Presidio, boy."

San froze.

"But we're together," Jacob said.

The soldier scrutinized Jacob and San. "He your houseboy or something?"

"No, he's...." Jacob hesitated. *I could lie and say that San is my servant, so he'd be allowed to stay with me.* He glanced at his friend. *But his father is a rich merchant. Would San be insulted if I claimed he was my servant?*

Just then, the boys heard a commotion inside the large tent. Loud barking was followed by high-pitched squealing and a man shouting. The soldier hurried inside.

Jacob looked around, but his dog was nowhere to be seen. "That's Quake!" he yelled and dashed inside the tent.

In the dim light, Jacob could see dozens of children playing and sitting on blankets. On one side, women with rolled-up shirtsleeves served food out of large pots. Jacob almost collided with a big, bony soldier who held Quake by the scruff of his neck. The dog squirmed and made choking sounds.

"Hey, let go of him!" Jacob hollered. "That's my dog!"

The soldier ignored Jacob.

"You're choking him! Put him down! What are you gonna do?"

The soldier stopped and scowled at Jacob. "I'm gonna shoot this mutt," he said. "It ran in here twice, and twice I booted it out. We can't have no stray dogs in here. Can't risk a sick animal runnin' loose around all these kids."

"He's not sick." Jacob planted himself in front of the big man. "You can't shoot him—he's my dog!"

"Jes' you watch me, kid," the soldier said. "Outta my way!"

Balling up his hands into fists, Jacob got ready to spring, but someone pushed him aside. It was the soldier who had greeted Jacob at the entrance.

A big bony soldier held Quake by the scruff of his neck.

"Give the kid his dog, John. No need to shoot it."

"Dog keeps runnin' in here. It ain't safe—a mangy mutt in here with all these kids. Fer all I know, it's got rabies," said John.

"Ever see a rabid dog?" asked the other soldier.

John frowned and shook his head.

"Well, they foam at the mouth and act vicious, crazy-like. Look, John, if this dog had rabies, he would've taken a hunk outta your arm by now."

John shoved the dog at Jacob. "Here," he growled. "You want this mutt, here it is. Don't let it loose in this tent again, though. You hear me?" He spit and walked off.

Jacob cradled Quake against his chest. The dog's whole body quivered.

The other soldier flicked his head toward the women serving food. "Go ahead and get yourself some dinner, kid. Just don't let your dog loose again."

"What about San?" Jacob asked.

"San? You mean that Chinese kid? I told you—he needs to go find his people. This tent's for Americans only."

Jacob glared at the soldier and stormed outside.

"San?" Jacob called. He looked around.

San edged out of a grove of trees near the tent's entrance.

Jacob hurried to him. "Come on," he said. "There's nothing for us in there."

Quake twisted and fidgeted, but Jacob held him firmly as he marched up the path. He wanted to put as much distance as he could between them and those soldiers. San trailed along behind them in silence.

The night was pitch-black, but little campfires guided the boys across the grounds. As soon as they were well away from the tent, Jacob set Quake down. The dog immediately ran up to one of the cooking fires and sniffed at the steam drifting from a pot.

"No, fella," Jacob called. "Come back! Quake, c'mere!"

Ignoring Jacob, Quake approached the stout woman who was stirring the pot. He nuzzled her free hand.

The woman chuckled. "Well, look who's come to dinner! Are ye always such a friendly pooch, or is it yer empty belly that makes ye so sweet-natured?"

She looked at San and Jacob. "I'm guessin' yer bellies are empty, too! Where's yer families, boys?"

"We don't know, ma'am. We came out here to look for them." Jacob approached the fire, but San hung back.

"Sure, and there's no need to be shy," the woman called to San. "We all got the same amount of nothin' out here."

San took two steps closer. The woman nodded cheerfully at him. "I already fed my man and the wee ones," she said. "He's rockin' 'em to sleep in there," she pointed to a ragtag tent made of blankets and skirts. "Might as well set down and have yerself a bit to eat. Sure, and there's no use in me cookin' all this food if it isn't gonna get eat up."

The boys looked at each other, then sat down. She handed them bowls of soup, thick with meat and vegetables. Jacob briefly wondered what kind of meat it was, but he was too hungry to resist.

The woman ladled a little soup into a third bowl and placed it in front of Quake. Then she looked at Jacob and San. "How'd ye get separated from yer people, boys?" she asked.

Between mouthfuls, Jacob and San repeated their stories.

"When I learned that Oakland is safe, my hope blossomed," San finished. "Now I believe my uncle took my mother and brothers there, and they are safe in my father's care. But until I am certain, I will keep searching for them."

"Well, if ye don't sound like an honest-to-God professor!" the woman said, beaming at San. When she smiled, her eyes crinkled and her front teeth gleamed in the firelight. "Has anybody told ye that they've set up a tent for children such as yerselves what can't find their folks?"

As soon as she mentioned the orphans' tent, both Jacob and San fell silent. San stared at the campfire, and Jacob chewed his lip.

"Now where'd those long faces come from?" the woman asked as she stroked Quake. "Cat snatched yer tongues all of a sudden?"

"We've already been to that tent," Jacob said. "One of the soldiers grabbed Quake. He was going to shoot him."

"Ye don't mean to say!" the woman exclaimed.

"And he told San he had to go to the Presidio," Jacob said.

The woman peered at San.

"The soldier told me the tent was for American children only," San said, his voice flat. "Chinese not welcome."

"Well, if that don't beat all! Anybody with ears would know ye're American, same as the rest of us." The woman leaned forward and gently cupped San's chin in her big hand. "Ye wouldn't go and get yerself all upset over somethin' a big bully said, would ye?"

San blinked back tears. "A thousand thanks, ma'am. You are a friend of the Chinese people."

"Oh, don't be thankin' me. I haven't said nothin' but God's honest truth!" The woman patted San's shoulder. "From now on, if anybody gives ye any trouble, tell 'em to come and speak to me—Annie Flanagan." She shook her fist in the air.

San smiled.

"Ye don't believe me? Well, wait 'til my man comes out here. If there's anything Kevin Flanagan won't abide, it's a bully. Sure there's no excuse to push a fella around just 'cause he comes from somewhere different. Like my husband says, 'We all gotta come from somewhere.'"

Hearing movement from the tent, Annie turned around. Her face broke into a broad smile. "Well, here's Kevin in the flesh. So I guess he'll be tellin' ye himself."

"That I will," boomed a voice with a heavy accent. As Kevin Flanagan approached the fire, Jacob and San opened their mouths in amazement. He was the tallest man either of them had ever seen.

A grin spread across the man's square face. Holding out an arm as thick as a tree branch, he shook hands with both boys. "Heard every word ye told the missus, boys. 'Tis a cryin' shame, it is, that our own soldiers treated ye so poorly. But I want ye to know the both of ye are welcome to stay here with Annie and me while ye look for yer people."

CHAPTER 11
CAMP FLANAGAN

Jacob heard the twitter of birds and smelled food cooking. When he opened his eyes, sunlight was glittering through the treetops. Quake nuzzled his face. Pushing the dog away, he sat up, blinking.

A few steps away, a red-haired boy spooned food out of a bowl. Annie Flanagan stood by the fire holding a bottle, and Kevin was bouncing a baby in his thick arms. A tiny freckle-faced girl who looked about four years old was leaning on San's knees. She held his long braid in her right hand and tried to tickle his neck with it. San pretended that he didn't notice, but he was grinning as he greeted Jacob.

Jacob stood up, brushing leaves and dirt off his clothes.

"Well, here's the last sleepyhead!" Annie wiped out a bowl and ladled some soup into it for Jacob.

Sitting cross-legged, Jacob began to eat. Quake stood in front of him, whining. A thin line of drool snaked out of the dog's mouth and dripped onto the ground.

"Now don't let yer dog talk ye outta yer breakfast," Annie said. "He's a sly one, that. I gave him a whole bowl for himself and then he lapped up Molly's leftovers, too."

Tucking the bottle under her arm, Annie held out her hands. Kevin handed her the baby. Annie sat down on an overturned bucket and guided the baby's hands around the bottle. As soon as the baby began making wet, smacking noises, Quake trotted over to investigate.

"I suppose ye'll go lookin' for yer people today?" Kevin asked.

The boys nodded.

Kevin told the boys where they'd find most of the campsites. "The park's shaped like a skinny rectangle," he said. "They say it's not but a half-mile wide. If a man walked straight west, he'd go maybe three miles before he'd see the ocean. Ye can even hear seals barkin' on them rocks offshore."

"People have been comin' in since daybreak," Annie said. "I have a hunch ye'll be findin' yer people today."

When the boys stood up to leave, Annie stopped them. "Promise me ye'll come right back here tonight if ye don't find yer people," Annie said. "As far as we're concerned, this camp is yer home now. Ain't that so, Kevin?"

The big man nodded, smiling.

The boys thanked the Flanagans, then Jacob called Quake and they set off. They walked around the eastern rim of the park, stopping to talk to everyone they saw. People gladly shared whatever news they had. The boys learned about the progress of the fire, about the dynamiting of buildings, and about the relief efforts. Everyone had a story to tell about where they were when the earthquake struck. The old-timers compared this disaster to earthquakes from years past.

But nobody had any information about the boys' families.

～

Around midday, Jacob and San approached a large group of people eating dinner on a blanket. The boys introduced themselves.

Quake hopped onto the blanket and padded up to a dark-eyed teenage girl. Wagging his tail, the dog lowered his haunches. The girl dangled a spaghetti noodle over the dog's head. When she released the noodle, Quake caught it in his mouth, gulped it down, and mopped his nose with his tongue. Everyone laughed. A young boy rose to his knees and held out another noodle. Quake repeated his performance, to the delight of his audience.

A middle-aged man sitting next to the little boy smoothed his dark mustache with his fingers. He had black hair, olive skin, and brown eyes. Jacob guessed he was the father of the boy and the teenage girl.

The man smiled at Jacob and San and introduced himself. "And this is the rest of the Torelli family," he said with a sweep of his hand. "Our home is—was—on Telegraph Hill."

Before Jacob and San could respond, the man began to tell them about how he'd almost managed to keep his home from burning. But when the wind changed direction, he had to give up the effort and run for cover. As he spoke, the man's hands danced in the air, turning and flapping to emphasize his meaning. Although he used English words, his accent was so thick that Jacob could barely understand the details of his story.

Jacob tried to listen, but his eyes kept straying to Quake, who was snapping up noodles as fast as they were dangled over his head. Jacob's stomach growled.

At last an elderly woman pushed herself off the blanket with a grunt. She waddled over to the pot and heaped steaming noodles into two bowls. She ladled some dark red sauce onto the spaghetti. Handing one bowl to Jacob and another to San, she urged them to eat with a word Jacob had never heard. It sounded like "Mahn-jay, mahn-jay!"

After thanking the family for dinner, the boys resumed their search. They introduced themselves to at least thirty groups of campers. By the time they reached the northern side of the park, daylight was beginning to fade.

"Maybe we should go look somewhere else?" Jacob suggested. Several people had told them that refugees were also being housed at the Presidio and Fort Mason, the two military reservations on the northern tip of the San Francisco peninsula. "Remember that soldier in front of the orphan children's tent? He said most of the Chinese went to the Presidio."

"How could I forget him?" San asked, frowning. "But it is better for us to stay here." He looked at Jacob. "Your family must be searching for you, and if you keep moving, how will they find you? I don't think my family is at the Presidio, anyway. I believe they're in Oakland. And if we leave Golden Gate Park, where will we sleep tonight? The Flanagans were kind enough to invite us to return to their camp."

"I guess you're right." Jacob whistled for Quake, and they started back to the Flanagan's campsite.

～

The next morning was Saturday, and Jacob awoke to shouts and whoops. He sat up and rubbed his eyes. "What's going on?" he asked.

"The fire's out!" Annie Flanagan announced. "Bless Jesus, it's finally over!" Tears were streaming down her cheeks as she repeated the news. "Two men just came runnin' by. They said that the soldiers put out the last of it at quarter past seven this mornin'."

Kevin Flanagan had already left with a crew of volunteers to start cleaning up the city streets. Annie had heard that a relief committee was giving out food and water to refugees. She asked Jacob and San if they'd mind standing in the line to get supplies for their camp.

The boys joined a stream of people heading for the relief tent. By the time they got there, the line snaked around for quite a distance. Men and women were waiting patiently, some in everyday clothing and others in expensive suits and dresses. Small children skipped and played, and to one side, four boys tossed a ball. Jacob and San walked to the end of the line. As they passed people, they studied their faces, hoping to find someone they knew.

Quake wagged his tail as he brushed by people's legs. Many of them reached out to pat the dog's head, and others smiled or chirped a greeting to him. When Jacob and San took their place in line, Quake joined the boys playing ball. Each time a boy ran to catch a pass, the dog loped along beside him.

Jacob and San had been waiting for about twenty minutes when they heard a commotion at the back of the line. They turned around and saw a man with black hair shouting at an older woman. When she tried to put her hands on the man's shoulders, his voice rose and he pushed her aside. Wailing, she called after him, "Lorenzo, please! I beg you."

The man ignored her. He stomped through the line, his eyes boring straight into Jacob and San.

All the people around Jacob fell silent. The ball-playing boys stopped their game and edged closer to each other. Some of the women gathered up their small children and clasped them against their shoulders.

Quake left the ball players and ran at Lorenzo, barking at the man's heels and nearly tripping him.

"No, Quake, c'mere!" Jacob called. He hurried over and grabbed the dog. Quake scratched Jacob's arm as he struggled to get loose. But Jacob clamped him firmly against his chest. "Easy, fella. Take it easy," he muttered.

Lorenzo planted himself in front of San and clamped a meaty

hand onto the Chinese boy's shoulder. "You! Get your filth outta here!" he roared. Pointing a thick forefinger at San's face, Lorenzo glared at him. "You hear what I'm saying?"

San stared at the man, but he didn't speak.

"Hey, let go of him!" Jacob shouted. "You have no right to tell him to get out of line. San's my friend."

Keeping his hand on San's shoulder, Lorenzo whirled to face Jacob. "Watch what you're saying, kid. Your mamma know you're hangin' around with this yellow boy? You know what kind of diseases you can catch from his kind? They live like animals. You can smell their filth a mile away."

"Lorenzo, I beg you," the older woman pleaded. She was panting from running to catch up. She clasped Lorenzo's arm with two bony hands. "Hot temper, always, the hot temper. You father always says you gonna get yourself in trouble with you hot temper."

"Mamma, we got no food, no drink. You expect me to stand back there and watch an animal get food first? You think people are sending these supplies here to feed vermin like him?"

The woman's face crumpled, and she began to cry. "Be a good boy, Lorenzo. What you want to cause trouble for?"

"Always the same—be a good boy, Lorenzo." The young man pointed at his throat. "You think I'm gonna be a good boy if I shut my mouth and watch this vermin eat up all the food, while our children starve?" He gestured at the other people in line. "You think they want him in this line? Mixing with their babies? No! I'm only saying what everybody thinks."

Jacob glanced at the other people in line. But nobody met his eyes. Their eyes shifted down to the ground, at their hands, or they gazed off into the distance.

"We're here to pick up food and water for our camp," Jacob said to Lorenzo. "We have as much right as anybody else."

Lorenzo sneered with disgust. "Your camp? A white boy living in a nest of Chinamen? Where's your own people, kid?"

"I'm living with the Flanagans, and so is San. They're taking care of us. And they have three little children to feed. They need food and water too," Jacob said.

"See, Lorenzo," said the older woman. "This boy says the food is for an Irish family. So leave them alone."

Lorenzo gestured toward Jacob. "Then this kid can pick up the food." He turned to San and said, "If the Irish want to let this filth live in their camp, that's their problem. But I'm not gonna stand in line behind him." Lorenzo pushed San.

San glanced sideways at Jacob and hurried away. Jacob paused, undecided. He wanted to stay with San, but he didn't want to give up his place in line. The Flanagans needed the supplies, and somebody had to get them. "Tell Annie I'll be back soon," he called to San.

San nodded quickly. Then he disappeared into the trees.

As soon as San was out of sight, Lorenzo sauntered to the back of the line. His mother bustled off behind him.

Jacob looked at the faces of the people near him, but they pretended that nothing had happened. Women put down their small children. Conversations started up again. The small boys resumed their ball game, but Quake didn't run off to join them. Instead, he stayed close to Jacob's side.

As the line inched forward, Jacob thought about the boys who had beaten San up at the candy store and the soldier who had kicked him out of the orphans' tent. He turned to the woman behind him and said, "Somebody ought to tell Lorenzo that he can't have supplies if he's gonna push around other people."

The woman looked at Jacob but didn't speak.

Jacob raised his eyebrows and stared at her. "You don't agree with what he said, do you?"

The woman shifted uncomfortably. "There are things you're too young to understand, sonny," she mumbled and looked away.

Jacob glared at her, then he exhaled loudly enough for her to hear. Turning away, he inched forward.

When he finally got to the front of the line, the scowl on his face startled the relief worker. She asked him if there was anything wrong, but Jacob just shrugged and thanked her for the loaf of bread and bucket of water.

As he started back to camp, Jacob saw a group of people gathered around a spry little man. He was talking nonstop. "Now ain't this somethin'?" the man said. "They're shippin' in supplies from everywhere—Los Angeles, Oakland, Denver. I hear they're already taking up collections for us in New York and Boston. That's America for you!"

Jacob listened for a moment, then elbowed his way through the crowd and approached the little man. "Excuse me, sir. Do you think somebody could send a message to Oakland? If food shipments are coming in from across the bay, then—"

"No problem, sonny!" the man said. "Just write your letter and drop it in that barrel over there." He pointed to a wooden barrel by the relief tent.

"But we have no money for a postage stamp," Jacob said.

"Don't need one. They're deliverin' letters for free."

Jacob hurried back to the Flanagans' camp. He couldn't wait to tell San about the mail barrel. Maybe this would make him feel better after his terrible treatment from that Lorenzo man.

He found San sitting under a tree on the path that they had taken to the relief tent.

Quake wagged his tail and nosed San's face. Jacob started to ask why he hadn't gone back to camp, but San held up his hand. "I do not want Annie to know about what happened in the relief line," he said.

"But San, you remember what Annie said after that soldier—"

"Yes, I remember," San said, his eyes fixed on a leaf that he twirled between his fingers. "And I know that Annie will tell Kevin what happened. Then Kevin will find Lorenzo and tell him to leave me alone, and they'll start arguing. Don't you see what will happen? The trouble this will bring?"

Jacob started to protest. "But it's not right for..."

San looked at him, and Jacob's words dried up. The hurt in his friend's eyes took away Jacob's breath.

Nodding quickly, Jacob said, "All right, I won't say anything to Annie or Kevin."

San stood up and brushed the dirt off his clothing. As they started to walk, Jacob told him about the mail barrel.

In an instant, San's face softened. "Are you sure?" he asked.

"That's what the man told me. And he showed me the mail barrel."

They told Annie about the mail barrel as Jacob handed over the bread and bucket of water.

"What can I do for paper?" San asked, his voice quivering with excitement. "And an envelope?"

"There's no need for an envelope if ye write a postcard," Annie suggested.

They all looked around the camp for a scrap of paper or cardboard, but found nothing suitable. Then Jacob had an idea. "You could use my shirt as paper," he offered. "It's white— well, almost white. I'm sure your father will be able to see the writing."

"A thousand thanks, Jacob." San chuckled. "But I cannot accept the shirt off your back."

"I'll still have the shirt on my back!" Jacob said. "Watch." Jacob stood up and slipped his shirt over his head. Holding the collar in his right hand, he balled the rest of the fabric in his left and tugged. The collar tore loose.

Jacob grinned as he handed it to San. "Here, this can be your postcard!"

The boys hurried back to the food distribution center to ask a Red Cross volunteer if they could borrow a pen and ink. San carefully printed his father's name and the address of his uncle in Oakland on one side of Jacob's collar. On the other side, he wrote a short message:

I am in G.G. Park—eastern edge.
Staying with Kevin Flanagan's family.
Your son.

Then he dropped the collar into the mail barrel.

～

On Sunday morning rain pelted down, soaking the refugees' tents and turning their cooking fires into charcoal puddles. The boys resumed their search after breakfast, but the miserable weather dampened everybody's spirits.

The first person they approached was an elderly woman curled up under an umbrella and holding a baby wrapped in a blanket on her lap. "Isn't this something?" she said to them. "If we'd gotten this rain a couple of days ago, it would've put the fire right out!"

For the next hour Jacob and San wandered up and down drippy paths. They passed dozens of makeshift camps, all looking somber and depressing in the rain. Most of the refugees huddled inside their crowded, leaky tents, taking whatever shelter they could from the steady downpour outside.

Eventually the boys found themselves on a circular road running past a large stucco building. Tall columns lined the front wall.

"What's that?" Jacob called to a man hurrying by.

"Memorial Museum," the man said, holding a newspaper over his head to keep off the rain. "Never been there? It's full of paintings and artwork. Egyptian mummies, stuffed birds—all sorts of things. Used to be real nice, but I hear they ain't letting anybody in there now. The earthquake wrecked the place," he said, moving on. "It's a real shame."

Jacob could see that the building was badly damaged. Chunks of the roof had peeled off and fallen to the ground, and some of the columns were broken. The lawn around the museum was littered with bricks and pieces of glass.

Curious, the boys walked up to the battered entranceway, but they couldn't see anything inside. A gust of wind blew the rain into Jacob's face. Water rolled down his neck and plastered his shirt against his back. He shivered. The ruined museum looked as gloomy as he felt. He was weary of searching, weary of telling his story over and over to strangers.

"Are you ready to call it quits for the day?" he asked San.

San looked at his cloth shoes and nodded. "My feet are soaking wet."

When they got back to the Flanagans' tent, they found Annie and the children inside. Annie was rocking the baby on her lap. As soon as Molly and her brother Sean saw Quake, the children begged Annie to let them go outside to play.

"In this rain?" Annie shook her head. "You'll end up lookin' like a pair of mudpies."

Little Molly clapped her hands to get Quake's attention. The dog darted inside the tent and shook off, spraying droplets of water in every direction. Sean screwed up his face in disgust, but Molly laughed aloud. Even though Quake smelled like wet, dirty wool, Molly hugged his head and let him nuzzle her face and lick her ear. After a few seconds, she squeezed her shoulder against her damp ear and scampered behind Jacob.

"Doggy wants to kiss me!" she said.

Jacob remembered Sophie playing like this when he'd first brought Quake home, and the musty smell inside the tent reminded him of the creaky old stairway in their boardinghouse. It had been a gloomy day just like this one when Mamma died in that cramped apartment. Jacob felt exhausted, as tired as he could ever remember.

"Don't be pesterin' these boys, Molly," Annie said. "Can't ye see they're half drowned from the rain?" She stood up and grabbed two blankets. "Here, Jacob, San. Get rid of those wet shirts before ye catch yer death of cold. Wrap up in these blankets 'til ye get warm."

~

The dry weather was back on Monday. But it didn't bring Jacob or San any better luck locating family or neighbors.

Camp life began to fall into a routine. At daybreak every morning Annie started cooking breakfast. Kevin ate quickly, then left with the crews of men going into the city to clean up. All able-bodied men were expected to help with the repairs. He said their first task was to replace the damaged water pipes. Until San Francisco had dependable water service again, the threat of another fire worried everybody. No indoor cooking was allowed, even in the houses that hadn't been damaged.

Every morning San helped Annie get the little ones dressed and fed. The boys never explained why Jacob always volunteered to go stand in the relief line. Whenever the topic was brought up, San seemed to have his hands full of dishes or he was busy feeding the baby his bottle or doing some other chore. Jacob brought back drinking water, milk, bread, and cans of food. Sometimes the relief committee volunteers handed out used clothing, too.

In the afternoons, the boys continued searching the park. After the experience with Lorenzo, San hung back while Jacob approached each new campsite. If the people seemed friendly and welcoming, then San edged closer as Jacob talked with them. But if they didn't acknowledge San with a nod or a smile, then he drifted off to a safe distance and waited until Jacob finished his conversation.

While they were wandering among the campsites one afternoon, Jacob and San spotted a hand-lettered sign tacked on a piece of tin serving as the roof of a ramshackle dwelling. "Cheer up," the sign said. When they got back to camp, the boys told Annie about it. A big smile spread across her sunburned face.

"Good advice, don't ye think?" she said.

After that, the boys made a point of noticing signs that were springing up all over the campsites. San found one that read "Camp Contentment." Another said "God Bless Our Home." And still another imitated the name of a local landmark, "Hotel St. Francis."

One evening, Kevin brought a small piece of board back from the city. He asked the boys to write "Camp Flanagan" on it. Then he hung it on a tall bush in front of their campsite.

CHAPTER 12
RATS AND GHOSTS

Rats?" Jacob and San stared at Kevin as the big man shared the day's news between mouthfuls of his supper.

"That's right, lads. Rats. The city's payin' a bounty for 'em," Kevin mopped up the last of his stew with a hunk of bread.

"Why rats?" Jacob asked.

"Been some cases of bubonic plague. A rat is a filthy animal what spreads disease. The city's offerin' five cents fer every rat brought in," Kevin said. "So, would ye lads be willin' to go downtown with me in the mornin'? I could use yer help."

Jacob and San raised their eyebrows and glanced at each other. "I'm willing to give it a try," Jacob said. "How about you, San?"

San nodded. "Sure, I'll go. And Quake is very good at catching rats," he said. "Remember the rat in Chinatown?"

Jacob smiled. "Yeah, Quake's pretty quick. Especially when he's hungry."

"Now hold on, lads," Annie said, and she turned to Kevin. "Don't ye think it'd be better to leave the pooch here? If it's true what ye say, that the plague spreads from fleas on the rats, we wouldn't want Quake gettin' anywhere near the varmints."

"Annie's right, we'll leave the dog here. We won't be touching the rats ourselves, o'course. We'll use sticks to pick up the dead bodies and drop 'em into a bucket of kerosene. The health department collects 'em 'til ten in the mornin'. After that, ye can take a walk about. Lots of folks have set up camp on the streets of their old neighborhoods. Ye may have some luck trackin' down yer families."

The boys woke early the next morning and ate a quick breakfast. Annie held Quake so he wouldn't follow as they hurried off. Jacob and San had to jog to keep up with Kevin's long strides.

At the eastern edge of the park a group of men were waiting for a ride into town. A few of the men frowned at San and muttered to each other, but they dropped their eyes when Kevin gave them a hard look. Soon, a horse-drawn wooden wagon clattered up, and everybody climbed aboard. Jacob and San sat down on either side of Kevin.

The wagon rumbled through the Western Addition, the large neighborhood between Van Ness Avenue and Golden Gate Park. All of the streets in this neighborhood were passable, even though some of the houses were damaged. The boys noticed cracked stucco walls, roofs with gaping holes, and crumpled balconies lying in heaps on the ground.

The damage was much worse when they reached Van Ness Avenue. Jacob felt like he was entering the ruins of an ancient civilization. The mansions on the western side of the broad avenue were still standing, but the army had blown up most of the buildings on the eastern side. Dusty mounds of rubble and jagged sections of wall were all that remained. Jacob glanced up the street toward the spot where the Merrill Mansion once stood. Less than a week ago he'd been inside that house—the closest he'd ever come to entering a palace—and now it was gone.

The wagon pulled to a stop in front of the tent set up by the health department, and Kevin and the boys jumped off. Kevin picked up a bucket of kerosene, then he led the boys along the avenue and down a side street. "We'll check the trash barrels first," he said. "That's where we're likely to spot the varmints."

Jacob and San listened for scuffling inside the barrels. If they heard noises, they overturned the barrel and pounded on its sides. When the rats came scuttling out, Kevin whacked them with a board. The boys used two sticks to pick up the furry lumps and drop them into their bucket. In less than two hours it was full of dark, shiny rat bodies.

Jacob strained to lift the heavy bucket. But Kevin grabbed it up in one of his big hands. When they got back to the tent, a health department worker counted the dead rats and paid Kevin cash.

"How much did you get?" Jacob asked.

"A dollar and fifteen cents. Now if ye ask me, that's a good day's work!" Kevin grinned and slapped Jacob's back. "Want yer share now, lads, or would ye rather wait 'til we get back to camp?"

Jacob and San exchanged glances, then San said, "We would like you to keep our share of the money. It is the least we can do to repay your kindness."

"That's mighty generous, lads. I'm thinkin' the money will come in plenty handy at Camp Flanagan whenever the stores open again."

Jacob and San trotted to keep up with Kevin as he headed east toward downtown. Some streets were so pitted and littered with bricks that they were nearly impossible to walk through. On many blocks there was hardly a building left standing. Here and there a chimney or a thin section of brick foundation jutted up like a spire in an empty field.

The air smelled bitter, like the last embers of a campfire. Jacob noticed thin wisps of smoke rising above the piles of

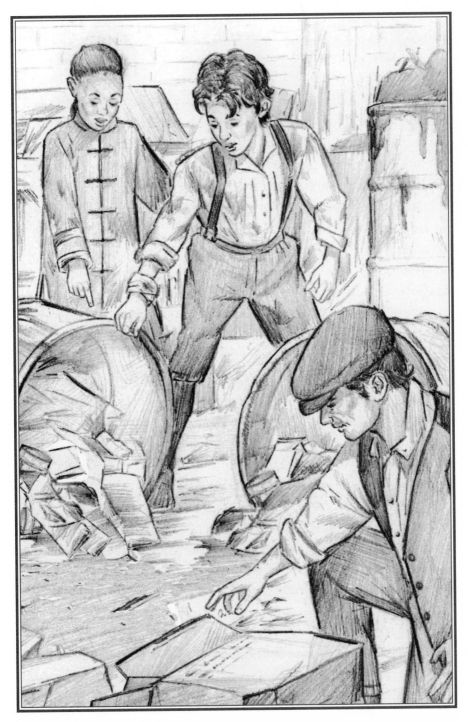

Jacob and San listened for scuffling inside the barrels.

ashes. "I thought they put out all the fires on Saturday," he said.

"As hot as that fire got, them ashes will be smoulderin' fer awhile," Kevin said.

Jacob had expected the ruins to look ugly and black, the way charcoal looks in an old fire pit. But under the clear white morning sun, the rubble gleamed pink and tan and lavender. He was surprised that the burned-out city seemed calm, almost beautiful.

Near Union Square, the St. Francis Hotel was still standing, massive above the sea of wreckage around it. Kevin left the boys in front of the square after giving them directions about where to meet one of the wagons returning to Golden Gate Park.

The boys were close to Chinatown, so they decided to go there first. With so many of the city's landmarks gone, it was difficult to tell one street from another. But as soon as Jacob recognized the shell of St. Mary's Church, he knew they were approaching San's neighborhood.

A few families were living in odd little shacks on the edge of the debris. They had built them with tin sheets, stray boards, and other material salvaged from the ruins. Clothing hung like curtains across the openings to provide a little privacy. Dotting the sidewalk were small stoves made of bricks and pieces of pipe.

The boys circled a few blocks, then San came to a stop. Checking his location by glancing at the church, he began to clamber over a heap of ash and rubbish. When he came to a depression in the heap, he knelt to examine it.

"What's that?" Jacob asked, joining him.

"Where I might have been buried if you and Quake did not find me."

Jacob was speechless. As his eyes wandered across the wreckage, he remembered that hundreds of people had been trapped in burning buildings. Some of them had died. *Bodies might be lying underneath the ground that I'm standing on!* Jacob thought, and he hurried back to the street.

San caught up with him and they walked on in silence. At the next corner, they saw five elderly Chinese men seated by a makeshift stove. San called out a greeting that sounded like "Knee how." The men answered with a stream of staccato syllables.

After a brief conversation, San waved good-bye to the men. "They say they've been out here since Sunday," he told Jacob, "and they've spoken to many people. But they haven't seen or heard about my uncle or my mother."

From Chinatown, the boys looked to the east. In the distance, they could see the remains of the Hall of Justice, which resembled the tall, crumbly pillars of an ancient Roman building. Its dome, now a metal skeleton, dangled off its top. To the right of this landmark, Jacob pointed out the Christmas tree–shaped roof of the Ferry Building. Beyond it, they could see the tall masts of ships in the harbor and glints of sunlight on the water.

Picking their way through the wreckage, Jacob and San found themselves on the Montgomery block downtown. The old buildings on this block were almost undamaged, even though they were in the heart of the burned-out area.

They headed down to Market Street through streets that were practically deserted. Some of the city's famous landmarks had completely vanished, but others stood sturdy and solid. Looking skyward, with the high Call-Spreckels Building on one side and the blockier Mutual Savings Bank across the street, Jacob could almost imagine that the disaster had never happened. But when he glanced down the street at City Hall, the lavish building that had cost the city millions of dollars, he gasped.

"Look, San!"

San followed Jacob's gaze. All of City Hall's columns and

walls had peeled off, leaving only a steel frame and a squat dome.

"A birdcage," San said.

"Huh?"

"City Hall," San explained. "It looks like a very large bird-cage."

The comparison made Jacob smile. "You're right. A big bird-cage with a round woolen cap on top."

Crossing to the south side of Market, the boys entered Jacob's neighborhood. The last time Jacob had seen these streets, many of the rickety boardinghouses had already collapsed into heaps of board and rubble. The fire had completed their destruction.

As they walked down Howard Street, Jacob saw pale smoke rising from ashes, like ghosts wavering above a graveyard. Only a week ago people and horses hurried through these streets, shopkeepers sold their goods, and children played. Now the world where he was born, the only home Jacob had ever known, was a shadow—a memory with no resemblance to the real things around him. A feeling of panic gripped him, and he began to run.

When he reached the site of his family's boardinghouse, Jacob slowed down and took a deep breath. The stink from the wreckage made him feel sick to his stomach.

People had erected little shacks along the edges of the street, like the ones in Chinatown. Jacob searched faces for someone he recognized. At last he spotted the cobbler who had a shop two doors from his boardinghouse.

"Mr. Straussberg!"

The man turned and squinted. "Who's that?"

"Jacob, Jacob Kaufman. Don't you remember me? I'm Itzak's son. You know, Itzak Kaufman, the butcher."

"Ah, Jacob. Of course." Mr. Straussberg smiled and patted Jacob's shoulder. "Good to see you. How's your family? Little

Sophie? She must have been scared to death when your building caved in."

Jacob stared at Mr. Straussberg.

The man's smile faded, and his eyes riveted on Jacob. "You don't mean to tell me that Sophie...? Oh, my God, no! Not your father? Oh, Jacob, I'm sorry!"

"I don't know, Mr. Straussberg." Tears began to slide down Jacob's cheeks. "I don't know what happened to them. I'm looking for them. That's why I'm here—to find them."

Mr. Straussberg pulled Jacob over to a small stove. "Here, sit down. I didn't mean to upset you. I'm sure your father is all right. When was the last time you saw him?" He offered Jacob some water. "A drink?" He pulled out a half of a loaf of bread. "Maybe a little bread? You must be hungry, eat. After you feel better, we can talk."

Jacob took a gulp of water, but his throat was so dry that he didn't think he could swallow the bread.

Glancing over Jacob's shoulder, Mr. Straussberg nodded in San's direction. "That Chinese kid who keeps hanging around here, you know him?"

San was standing in the middle of the street, one foot resting on a chunk of fallen chimney.

"That's San," Jacob said. He beckoned to his friend. "San Wei Chang. I met him after the earthquake. We're living together at Golden Gate Park."

"Well, if he's your friend, then tell him to come here and have something—water, a little bread."

The boys sat with Mr. Straussberg for a half hour. He told them that he'd returned to Howard Street the previous morning. Before that, he'd been staying with some people out on Castro Street. He said he'd be sure to let Itzak or Avi know where Jacob was if they did come by.

"Wait a minute," Mr. Straussberg said. "I've got a better idea. Why don't you make a sign? Print your name and where you're staying." He took a pencil out of his pocket.

Jacob hunted through the rubble for a usable scrap of wood. On it, he printed these words in large letters:

JACOB KAUFMAN
IS IN G.G. PARK, EASTERN END
LOOK FOR CAMP FLANAGAN

Mr. Straussberg helped the boys gather up bricks and stack them near the site of the boardinghouse where the Kaufmans used to live. Jacob mounted his sign securely on top.

The boys thanked Mr. Straussberg and said good-bye. As they started to walk back toward Market Street, Jacob turned around and reread the words he'd written. The sign was perched on a pillar of wreckage, but somehow it made him feel better. It was as if a message had sprouted out of the ashes, promising life and hope.

CHAPTER 13
A SHIRT STORY

By the time the wagon dropped Jacob and San at Golden Gate Park, it was late afternoon. They walked slowly back to the Flanagans' campsite, enjoying the feeling of soft earth under their feet. The park looked so alive, so green and comforting, after the stark ruins of the city.

As they rounded a bend in the path, Quake began to bark. Standing beside the Flanagans' tent were two men dressed in long silken tunics and dark pants. Their foreheads were shaved up to the edge of their round hats, and a long, skinny braid hung down each of their backs.

Jacob looked at San.

His friend's eyes were open as wide as his mouth. "Father?" San whispered.

One of the men turned, and San rushed to him.

"My son!" The man put out his arms and cradled San's head to his chest.

The smaller man lowered himself to his knees and bowed his head. "Forgive me, nephew," he wailed. "You did not return...we waited and waited, but there was such smoke, flames! People were pushing to get on board the ferry. I thought we would miss our chance to reach your father. I thought my sister and your little brothers were in terrible danger. Your mother, she kept begging me, 'Wait for San.' But I told her, 'No, no, I have to take you to Oakland. Think of your little ones.'"

He raised his head and looked at San. "I deeply regret this now, nephew. I should have returned, searched for you, but I thought…"

San leaned over and hugged his uncle. "I understand, Uncle," he said.

Jacob walked closer to the group. He could see something in the taller man's hand. It looked like…it was his collar! Jacob smiled, but his vision blurred and for a split second, he imagined that the men standing here were his father and Uncle Avi. A wave of sadness washed over him and sucked his breath away.

Quake pawed at San's pant leg.

"This is the dog that found me in Chinatown, after the doorway collapsed on me," San said. He turned and gestured toward Jacob. "And this is my friend, Jacob Kaufman. They saved my life, Father."

Mr. Chang greeted Jacob with a formal bow. Then, smiling, he looked in Jacob's eyes and held out his right hand. Jacob shook the man's hand.

"I am pleased and honored to meet you, Jacob Kaufman," said Mr. Chang. "I consider you a most esteemed friend of the Chang family."

San explained how Jacob had also lost his family and how the boys had helped each other after the earthquake.

Mr. Chang put his hands on Jacob's shoulders and thanked him over and over. "Please do me the honor of coming to Oakland with us, Jacob. You will be our honored guest as long as you wish."

San shook his head up and down eagerly. "Yes, Jacob, come with us. In a few weeks, when things are better, we can take the ferry back to San Francisco to search for your family." San turned to his father. "That would be all right, wouldn't it, Father?"

Mr. Chang nodded. "Of course."

Jacob looked at San, who beamed happily at him. *If I go to Oakland now, San's family will take care of me. There'll be food, a house to sleep in. I wouldn't have to be a burden to the Flanagans.*

But doubts rushed into his mind. *What if Papa comes here looking for me?* He pictured his father's face—the slender wrinkles around his eyes. He remembered how Papa had wept after Mamma died, and another wave of sadness filled him from head to foot. His legs felt so weak, he could hardly stand.

"I-I can't," Jacob stammered. "If Papa is—I mean—he must be worried sick about me. I don't want to leave San Francisco, not until I know if..."

Mr. Chang nodded. "Of course. You are a good son. Your father must be very proud of you." Turning to Annie, he offered to take the Flanagans over to Oakland and find them a place to live.

But Annie shook her head. "We thank ye for the kind offer, Mr. Chang. But there's gonna be plenty of work here for the likes of Kevin Flanagan. We'd best stick where we are. Who knows? Maybe when all this settles down, we'll have us a fine, new house in the city."

Before saying good-bye, San asked his father for the collar. He pressed it into Jacob's hand. "I return your collar with a promise, Jacob Kaufman—my father and I will come back and get you if...whenever you're ready. This is the address where I'll be in Oakland."

CHAPTER 14
KEEPIN' SPIRITS BRIGHT

Without San, Camp Flanagan felt strangely empty. Molly and Sean kept asking Jacob when he was coming back. Quake padded around the tent, sniffing and pawing like a mother dog searching for a lost puppy.

Two days after San had left for Oakland, Jacob was making his usual trip to the bread line when Quake started barking. A boy near the front of the line had a long braid and a jacket the same color as San's.

The resemblance was so striking that Jacob slipped out of line and rushed to the boy's side. "San!" he called. "San? Why are you here?"

As soon as the boy turned around, Jacob realized his mistake. He mumbled, "Sorry, I thought you were…you look like…"

Lowering his eyes, Jacob trudged to the end of the line.

That afternoon, Jacob didn't feel like going off by himself. Instead, he volunteered to mind the Flanagan children while Annie took their clothes to the pond for a much-needed rinsing.

Before her mother was out of sight, Molly turned to Jacob. "Wanna come to my tea party?" she asked.

Jacob winced. Tea parties were Molly's favorite pastime, and she begged him to play this game at least once a day. Usually he didn't mind, but this afternoon, he wanted to sit quietly with his own thoughts.

"I need to keep my eyes on the baby," he told Molly. "But I bet Quake is hoping you'll ask him."

A grin spread across Molly's face, and she pranced into the tent. When she came out, she was holding Annie's blue sweater, her own dirty yellow sunbonnet, and a blanket. Molly told Quake to sit, then she struggled to push his front paws into the sleeves of the sweater. The dog sat patiently, his tail swishing back and forth, as she fussed over him. When Molly's head got near his nose, he licked her eyelids. "Be a good lad," she said, giggling, "and sit still while Mummy gets you dressed."

At last Quake's paws were in the sleeves. Molly fastened the top button and tied the sunbonnet around the dog's head. Then she spread out the blanket and urged Quake onto it. The dog watched with eager eyes as Molly crumbled a hunk of bread into small pieces. As she fed little bits to him, she prattled, "Have yerself a bit to eat. Sure, and there's no use in me cookin' all this food if it isn't gonna get eat up."

Molly's chatter was a perfect imitation of Annie's, and Jacob had to cover his mouth to keep from laughing. After Quake had gobbled down the bread, Molly poured water into a cup for him.

While his sister was absorbed in her tea party, Sean busied himself building a fort with sticks and rocks. Jacob bounced the baby up and down on his knees, turning him first one way and then another so he could watch his sister and brother at play.

Before long, Sean grew tired of his project. He stood up and began to run back and forth, knocking his fort apart. "Watch out, here comes the earthquake!" he yelled.

Quake whined softly as he watched Sean. Finally, ignoring Molly's protests, the dog sprang to his feet and shook himself. The bonnet loosened and dangled off one ear.

Snatching a stick out of his fort's wreckage, Sean sent it sailing over the blanket. Quake leaped after it. Sean slapped his knees and called, "C'mere, Quake!" then he darted around the back of the tent.

Quake pawed off the sweater and chased after Sean. One of the strings from Molly's bonnet tangled around his leg, and the dog dragged it across the ground.

"No, Sean, stop it!" Molly hollered. When her brother ran out from behind the tent, she threw herself onto him and pummeled him with her fists. "Quake is having a tea party with me!"

Sean darted out of reach. "Is not!" he shouted. "You can't have a tea party after an earthquake."

"Yes, you can!" Molly shouted.

"Cannot," Sean taunted. "There's no such thing as a tea party outside—that's only a picnic. And there's no cooking allowed indoors after an earthquake. Besides, Quake's gotta go downtown with me—every able-bodied man has to help rebuild the city."

Molly burst into tears.

Jacob sighed. He went over and put the baby down on the blanket. "Excuse me, Miss Flanagan," he said to Molly. "My baby is very thirsty, and I hear you're having a tea party out here in the park. Do you think we could come?"

Molly hesitated, then curtsied and flashed a smile. "I was just heating a fresh pot," she said. "Why, that's a fine, strappin' baby, mister. Did I hear ye say yer name's Mr. Jacob?"

Jacob nibbled bits of bread and sipped water from a cup until he spotted Annie returning to camp. Then he jumped to his feet. "We're running low on firewood," he announced. "I'd better go get some before it's time to start supper." Turning to Molly, he said, "I appreciate the tea and bread, Miss Flanagan."

Molly started to object, but Annie put an end to it. "That's enough tea partyin' fer now, young lady. I'll be needing you to keep an eye on the baby while yer brother helps me spread these clothes out to dry." Winking at Jacob, Annie urged him to hurry up with the firewood.

That evening Kevin returned from town early. He was carrying three long planks. For the past week he had been bringing home scraps of lumber or sheets of tin that he'd salvaged from ruined buildings downtown. He and Jacob used the materials to make little improvements for their camp: a shelf for storing food, a stool to sit on.

While Annie got the little ones ready for bed, Jacob helped Kevin on his latest project—a sort of porch where the children could play and Annie could cook, even if the weather turned rainy. But with only odds and ends, it was taking more imagination than skill to figure out how to construct the addition.

After an hour of struggling with two mismatched sheets of tin for the roof, Kevin shook his head in frustration. Jacob suggested fastening the pieces together by cutting a slot near the edge of one sheet and a tab in the rim of the other.

"Well now, there's a clever notion." Kevin grinned. "With me big hands, I'd be poundin' and pushin' at these scraps until they weren't fit fer anything but the dustbin. But with yer sharp noggin', ye figured out how to do the job in two shakes of a lamb's tail!"

Jacob turned red, but he was pleased by the compliment. He wanted to be helpful to the Flanagans. Even though they had three small children to care for, they had taken him in. *What would I do if I hadn't found them?* The thought made Jacob feel lucky until he remembered his own family. Then sadness washed back over him like the tide.

~

The army began issuing sturdy tents to families living in the parks. Soldiers set them up on wooden platforms in orderly rows, like the streets of a little city. The Flanagans were delighted when they were allowed to move into one of them. It was much roomier than the makeshift tent they were using before.

A list of the people living in each tent was posted in front to help family members and friends locate each other. At Camp Flanagan, the list of occupants read:

Kevin Flanagan
wife—Annie Flanagan
children—Sean, Molly, and Baby Flanagan
Jacob Kaufman

Trainloads of supplies from all over the United States arrived daily in San Francisco. One afternoon Jacob volunteered to help empty a wagonload of canned goods. He carried cartons into a wooden storage building and stacked them next to sacks of potatoes, flour, oatmeal, and sugar.

While he was working, Jacob listened to the other volunteers talk about what was happening in the city. According to newspaper reports, thousands of people had left to take shelter in Oakland and other cities. And thousands more were living on San Francisco's streets and in parks.

Thousands, Jacob thought. *With so many people living on the streets and gone to other cities, how will I ever find Papa and Sophie?* But he kept checking the posted lists and searching for new tents in the park.

Jacob certainly wasn't the only one looking for missing family members. Every day people wandered through the campsites asking about this or that person. There were signs tacked up all over the park that requested information about lost relatives.

One afternoon little Molly sat chewing a piece of bread.

Suddenly she spit something into her hand. "Look!" She held out a folded piece of paper.

Jacob took the damp scrap and carefully unfolded it. The words on it were faded, but he could still make them out. "Have you seen my brother, Nathan Conley, or his family?" he read aloud. "Please contact Elizabeth Myers—Holden Lane, Los Angeles."

"If that don't beat all!" Annie said. Shaking her head, she examined the note. "This poor woman, so worried about her brother that she baked this note in a loaf of bread!"

Annie smoothed out the paper and laid it in a corner of the tent to dry. "We'll hang this on the camp's message board tomorrow," she said. "Whenever I get to feelin' sorry fer myself about havin' no roof over our heads, I'll think about this note. It'll remind me how lucky I am that all the Flanagans are right here, safe and sound."

As soon as the words were out of her mouth, Annie gasped. "Oh, listen to me, rattlin' on like that, with you sittin' right here. I'm sorry, Jacob. I don't know what I was thinkin'."

"It's all right," Jacob said, but he avoided her eyes.

Molly looked back and forth between her mother's face and Jacob's. Then she jumped up, circled behind Jacob, and licked his ear.

"Yow!" Jacob chuckled. "Why'd you do that, Molly?"

"To make you smile. That's how Quake makes me smile."

Jacob tickled Molly's neck. Squealing, she dashed around the side of the tent. "Can't catch me, can't catch me," she chanted in a singsong voice.

Jacob chased after her, but his heart wasn't in the game.

That night he had trouble falling asleep. He shifted uncomfortably on the hard floor of the new tent, trying not to disturb the sleeping Flanagans. *What if Papa and Sophie moved to*

another city and never come back? What if they're not...alive?
He tried to imagine a future without his family, but his stomach
knotted up and his thoughts scattered every which way, like
panicky rabbits.

He finally dozed, but he woke up sweaty in the middle of the
night. In his dream, he'd been walking toward the bread line
when he heard a little girl screaming. He began to run, faster
and faster, until he found himself on a dark street. Houses were
falling down in front of him, one after another, and he jumped
out of their way. Quake was running beside him, yelling at him
to hurry in a voice that sounded like San's.

Pushing off his blanket, Jacob listened to the sounds of crick-
ets and other night creatures. He felt so lonely, like he was adrift
on a boat in the middle of a vast sea. Quake padded over and
nosed his face. When Jacob turned onto his side, the dog curled
up next to him, his furry head resting on Jacob's arm.

～

In the morning Jacob woke early to go rat-catching with Kevin.
After they delivered their bucket to the health department work-
ers, Jacob went off on his own. He checked the street where
Uncle Avi lived, as well as the Meat and Produce Districts. Then
he returned to Howard Street and spoke with Mr. Straussberg.
But he didn't learn any news about Papa and Sophie or about
Avi's family.

As soon as he returned from the city, Annie put him to work
peeling potatoes for dinner. Jacob lingered over the last spud, cutting off the peel in a long curling ribbon for Molly's amusement.

Quake began to bark.

"That's his happy bark," Sean announced. "Daddy must be
home."

Sure enough, Kevin Flanagan turned the corner and strolled
up the dirt path between the tents. He was whistling.

Grinning, the big man rumpled Sean's hair and twirled Molly through the air. Then he pecked Annie on the forehead and brushed his fingers against the baby's cheek.

"I've brought a bit o' good cheer fer us," Kevin said, fishing a dirty scrap of paper out of his pocket.

"Only some paper," Sean said, his voice deflated.

"I jotted down a verse I saw on a downtown shack. Wait'll ye hear the words, son. They're just what the doc ordered fer keepin' spirits bright. Here, Jacob. Read it so we can all hear."

Jacob took the paper and read the verse aloud:

The cow is in the hammock
The cat is in the lake,
The baby in the garbage can,
What difference does it make?
There is no water, and still less soap
We have no city, but lots of hope.

Annie grinned and asked Jacob to read it again. When he finished, she had him call out each line slowly so they could repeat it. After a couple of times through, she made up a tune to go with the words. Soon the whole family was dancing around the tent, singing and laughing.

Seeing her mother so happy, little Molly spun round and round. Quake jumped to his feet and followed, barking like an excited puppy.

All the noise brought their neighbors, the Reillys, over. "What's going on here?" Mr. Reilly asked.

"It's Christmas!" Molly announced. "Isn't it, Mummy?"

"No, child, not Christmas," Annie said as she wiped her cheeks with her fingertips. "Just funny words. To keep our spirits bright, like Da said. Will ye read the poem again, Jacob?" She turned to Mrs. Reilly. "My tongue gets in a tangle when I'm readin' out loud. But ye should hear Jacob. He sounds like a regular stage actor, the words come so smooth out of his mouth."

Although Jacob knew his cheeks were red, he reread the poem. Immediately, Molly and Sean chimed in with the song that Annie had made up. The Reillys joined in on the last line. Before long, both families were slapping their thighs and laughing.

"I swear there ain't no better medicine than laughin'," Annie said. "That's what this city needs to get itself back on its feet."

Mr. Giannini, who lived with his sister's family across the way, peeked his head out of his tent and asked what all the commotion was about. A little crowd began to gather in front of the Flanagans' tent. Some of the neighbors brought musical instruments they'd saved from the fire—guitars, mandolins, flutes. Soon enough, a sing-along rang out over the tent village.

Jacob looked around. A few weeks ago these people were strangers who lived in different sections of the city, like members of separate tribes. They wouldn't have spent an evening in each other's company, singing and laughing. But out here in the dim light from the campfires, their smiling faces looked so similar that they might have been kinfolk.

Soon a sing-along rang out over the tent village.

CHAPTER 15
WAVES OF DOUBT

The next morning Jacob was standing in the bread line when he heard the news: An information bureau had been set up to help relatives find each other!

He picked up the supplies—two loaves of bread, a bag of coffee, and five cans of vegetables. Then he hurried over to the line where people were waiting to see the register of names.

The information bureau was only a small, open tent with a table, some chairs, and a large book. A tall woman sat by the table, her brown hair rolled up around her ears like a sausage and gathered into a plump bun in the back. As each person stepped to the front of the line, the woman smiled, asked a few questions, and thumbed through the register.

Jacob waited more than an hour before he finally got his turn. As he introduced himself to the tall woman, Quake nosed the hem of her skirt.

"What a friendly dog!" she said, stroking Quake's back. "I bet he makes your tent feel more like home."

Jacob smiled as he set the cans on the ground and balanced the loaves and bag of coffee on top of them. "I'm looking for my family," he told her. "My father's name is Itzak Kaufman. And I have one uncle—Avram Kaufman."

"Spell the last name, please."

The woman leafed through the thick book. Jacob watched the pages riffle by, each filled with names in alphabetical order—

a sea of names. The woman looked up. "Nobody here by that name. Sorry."

"Maybe you have an Isaac Kaufman?" he asked. "That's the American way to say Itzak. Or an Abraham Kaufman?"

The woman ran her index finger up and down a page of names. "No. But I see two Joseph Kaufmans. And here's a Morris Kaufman. Are you related to them?"

Jacob shook his head. He could feel his throat begin to tighten. Quickly he turned away.

"Wait a minute," she called. "Don't leave until I add your name to my list."

While the woman wrote down his name and where he was staying, Jacob gave his eyes a quick swipe with the back of his hand. He got up to leave.

"Hold on." The woman pointed to the supplies on the ground. "You wouldn't want to forget these."

As Jacob reached for the groceries, the woman touched his shoulder gently. "Don't give up, all right? We're adding new names to the register every day."

Back in camp, Jacob handed Annie the loaves of bread. He stacked the cans and coffee on the shelf that he and Kevin had built from scrap wood.

While Annie prepared lunch, Jacob told her about the register. "No luck," he said. "I even had her look up the American spelling of Itzak."

"How about Kaufman?" Annie asked. "Can Kaufman be spelled different?"

Jacob stared at her. "I didn't think of that." He broke off a piece of bread and waved as he ran off. "I'll be back soon."

The tall woman greeted Jacob with a kind smile. She agreed to search for the name Koffman. But there were no Itzaks or Isaacs, Avrams or Abrahams under Koffman either. She even tried looking under the Cs.

When that didn't help, she suggested that Jacob return in a few days. "Remember, we're adding new names every day," she said. "We'll locate your family. It's just a matter of time."

Jacob nodded and forced himself to smile as he said good-bye. But he left the tent feeling more discouraged than he had since the day of the earthquake.

Whistling for Quake, he began wandering through the camp-sites, hoping to spot a new tent that might mean Papa and Sophie had recently been relocated to this park. After a while, he reached the end of the refugee camps. But he kept walking, letting his thoughts roam.

The afternoon sun was slanting through the trees when he found himself at the western end of the park. The salty breeze made his skin tingle. In front of him was the vast, gray Pacific Ocean, its waves booming against the shore.

Quake raced to the edge of the water and barked at the sea-gulls. Squawking, the gulls wheeled into the sky and landed far-ther up the beach. The dog chased after them, then turned and scampered back to Jacob, his paws kicking up clods of wet sand.

Jacob sat on a rock and stared at the waves rolling in from the sea. He thought of the strange, unnerving feeling of the earth moving beneath him during the earthquake. The deep, constant motion of the waves seemed to lift him outside his surroundings and wash him deep inside his mind.

He thought about his neighborhood, once bustling with busi-ness, with people. He pictured the bruised face of Timothy's drowned grandmother, and icy prickles of panic rippled across his skin. He remembered his first look at San, when his friend had emerged from the collapsed doorway, covered with white dust. Jacob remembered how surprised he was when San shook off the dust and revealed that he was a boy, not an old man.

He let his thoughts wander back to his family. Smiling, he pictured Uncle Avi's kind, homely face. And Sophie—how her eyes had sparkled that evening when Jacob brought Quake home! It seemed to Jacob that during the past year his life had been churned and pounded, like a grain of sand below the ocean. His thoughts drifted to Mamma, to her white and silent face as she lay on the soiled sheets. The memory was so sharp that Jacob felt as if he was right there beside her on the day she died. In his mind, he traced her features—her eyebrows rumpled by the pillows, her lips slightly parted, her tangled hair stuck to her neck and forehead. He saw Papa cradling her limp hand, and he watched tears course slowly down the man's ashen cheeks.

So many months separated Jacob from that awful day. But looking back, he thought he could see more than what had actually happened, more than just outward events. Jacob felt he could peer inside his father, examine the man's emotions, watch Papa's enthusiasm bleed away with his tears.

Jacob remembered how angry he'd gotten on the night before the earthquake, when Papa had refused to let him keep the dog. Now Jacob wondered why he had been so upset, why he had shouted. *Why didn't I go to Papa and wrap my arms around his chest?* All it would have taken was a word or two and he could have made his father understand. And then he wouldn't have left the house so early, wouldn't have been in the street when the earthquake struck, wouldn't have lost his family...

Jacob sighed. *I probably won't ever find out what happened to Papa and Sophie. I'm probably an orphan.* He shut his eyes and took a deep breath of salty air. He tried to imagine himself alone with no family, but the picture was blurry and disorienting—like fog rolling in from the ocean.

He knew it was time for him to decide what to do. His life had changed, he couldn't make time go backwards. And he couldn't stay in Camp Flanagan forever.

Of course, he should stay and help Annie and Kevin for the

next few weeks. They'd been so kind to him. But what would he do after that, after the city was rebuilt?

Jacob decided he'd return to school. He wasn't particularly big or strong for his age, but he was good at reading and schoolwork, clever at solving problems and picking up facts. Even though he wasn't sure how this could translate into a way to make a living, he felt confident that he'd work it out eventually.

But where would he live in the meantime? How could he support himself?

Jacob reached into his pocket and fingered the torn shirt collar that San had used as a postcard. *Maybe I could go live with San's family. I could offer to work after school at Mr. Chang's shop to earn my keep.* Jacob had only seen Chinese people working in Chinatown, but so what? If Mr. Chang had a Jewish stock boy, the novelty might increase his business.

Jacob didn't know how he'd be able to keep the kosher laws if he lived with the Changs, but he decided he could figure that out later. Going to the Changs' house felt like a good decision. *I'll write to San tomorrow,* he thought. *Let him know that I'll accept the offer to come live with them.*

Quake nuzzled Jacob's hands. When Jacob ignored him, Quake stretched out his front legs on the sand. The dog screwed up his face into his funny little grin and whined.

Jacob laughed. "I'm sitting here worrying about our future, but all you're worried about is your stomach!" He reached over and rolled Quake onto his back, then scratched his tummy. "You win, fella. I guess it's time to head back to camp."

Jacob stood and brushed sand off the seat of his pants. He'd been sitting in one position for so long that his legs felt stiff. Stretching, he took a last look at the waves. When he turned to walk back to camp, he felt taller and stronger—as if he'd shed his old, cramped skin and tossed his boy-self into the sea.

*Jacob sat on a rock and stared at the waves
rolling in from the sea.*

CHAPTER 16

THE WARM, SOFT LIGHT OF THE CAMPFIRE

As Jacob hurried through the park, he noticed a line in front of the storehouse. He stopped to ask a woman what the line was for, and she told him the Red Cross was handing out blankets. Jacob decided he might as well get in line. Molly and Sean had been sharing a blanket because Jacob was using their other one.

The line inched forward, and Jacob's stomach growled. Quake was unusually restless. He kept barking and he would not stay at Jacob's side. He sniffed the ground furiously and pushed through the legs of the people in front of Jacob. Several people turned and glared at Jacob, their eyebrows lifted.

"C'mere, fella," Jacob said. He held out his hand, but the dog skittered away, still barking. "Shhh, settle down. We'll get supper soon."

Barking even louder, Quake dashed to the side of the line just out of Jacob's reach. He crouched low, his rump in the air and his tail whipping back and forth like a flag in a hurricane. "Come, Quake," Jacob coaxed, edging closer. Jacob reached out to grab him, but the dog dashed up the line.

"Stupid animal!" Jacob muttered, shaking his head. He stepped back into line and tried to ignore the dog's barking.

From the sound of it, Jacob guessed Quake must have run all the way to the front of the line.

Suddenly he heard a squeal. "Fluffy! That's Fluffy, that's Jacob's doggy!"

Jacob froze. *I must be imagining things.*

"Uncle Avi, look—that's Fluffy! Remember? The doggy you gave Jacob."

Quake came charging through the line toward him, but Jacob had already started running. Near the front of the line a little girl was perched on the shoulders of a dark-haired man.

"Where'd the doggy go? Where'd Fluffy go, Uncle Avi?"

"Sophie!" Jacob shouted.

The little girl shrieked and squirmed off Avi's shoulders. She began to push through the line.

Quake reached Sophie first. He jumped on her, knocking her onto the ground. She scrambled to her feet, calling, "Jacob! It is you! We've looked everywhere for you!" She threw herself at her brother and wrapped her arms around his waist.

Jacob pried her loose and lifted her high into the air. He twirled her around and around, saying, "Sophie, Sophie." As he gathered her into a hug, he looked up at his uncle.

Avi held out his arms and drew both of them to his chest. Tears rolled down his cheeks. "You're alive, Jacob," he thundered. "Thank God! Thank God!"

Quake danced in and out of their legs, all the while yapping like a puppy. The people around them watched the family reunion. Some of them even cheered and clapped. Jacob smiled at them, then he burst into tears.

"Jacob, Jacob, where have you been? We looked high and low for you!" Avi said, his arms waving through the air. "Up and down Washington Street! South of Market, the Ferry Building—you name it. We've been to Fort Mason and all the way out to the Presidio. We came out here and checked the orphans' tent, but we didn't see any sign of you. I swear our footsteps made more holes in the streets than the earthquake! Your father is out of his mind with worry!"

"Papa!" Jacob gasped. "Is Papa all right?"

Avi looked at his nephew. "All right? He's afraid he's lost his only son." Then Avi smiled. "But now he'll be all right. Wait until he sees you! One look at you will do him more good than all the medicine in America!" Avi took Jacob's head in his hands and planted a big kiss on his nephew's forehead.

"Come on," Avi said, "we'll worry about blankets later. Your father is at our new campsite with Rose and the babies."

Sophie clutched Jacob's hand as they hurried across the darkening park. She chattered nonstop. "Auntie Rose says it was all Uncle Avi's fault we lost you. She said he shouldn't have given you the stupid dog, then you never would have gone away. But I told her Fluffy is a nice dog. Isn't he, Jacob? He isn't sick. He couldn't sleep, but that's because he wasn't used to being inside our house.

"Papa says he never should've let you go out alone in the dark. But the doggy would've been scared out there alone, wouldn't he, Jacob? And you are a big boy. Lotsa times you take me to the store. And Papa always tells me I should hold your hand because..."

Jacob had a million questions to ask—about how his father and Sophie managed to escape from the wrecked boardinghouse, how they'd found Avi's family, how long they'd been in Golden Gate Park.... And he was bursting to tell them about where he'd been, about finding San in Chinatown, and about the Flanagans taking him in.

But Sophie's chatter was like a cool stream running through his parched mind. He didn't want her to stop. He lifted her up by the arm and she took a flying leap through the air, squealing as her feet landed on the ground.

Letting go of Jacob's hand, she squatted down to hug Quake. The dog mopped her nose with his tongue, and Sophie exploded into delighted giggles.

Jacob looked at Avi. "I was afraid I'd never see..." His throat tightened.

Avi nodded. "I know, nephew. Believe me, I've been plenty worried, too. And my brother! Poor man can talk of nothing else but where Jacob can be, what could have happened to Jacob. I kept telling him we'd find you. Believe me, I was praying that my words would come true." Avi shut his eyes. "God is good."

As they neared a small campfire, a man stood up. Jacob sucked in his breath. He would have recognized that silhouette anywhere.

"Look, Papa! We found Jacob!" Sophie skipped toward the fire.

"It's true!" Avi called. "Jacob has come back to us, good as new. I think he's grown two inches—what a sight for sore eyes he is!"

Itzak rushed toward them, grabbed Jacob's shoulders, and stared at his son's face. For a long moment, neither spoke.

Quake whined and pawed at Jacob's pants leg. Jacob glanced at the dog. "Papa, I'm sorry," he said. "I disobeyed you. I meant to leave the dog on Washington Street, but—"

Encircling Jacob with his arms, Itzak rocked him back and forth. Jacob could feel his father trembling. In a husky voice, Itzak muttered, "My son, my son."

"I went back to find you," Jacob said. "It was terrible—broken stuff everywhere. Our whole house was gone, I was so scared that you and Sophie...I kept calling your names. Then I saw Timothy's grandmother. She was dead, and they carried her out on a board..."

Quake whined again. The dog's tail swished back and forth across the ground.

"Papa, I ate pork," Jacob blurted out. "I thought maybe I'd get sick if I refused to eat, so I broke the kosher laws. And I kept the dog, even though you told me to get rid of him. I knew I was disobeying you. But I couldn't...I won't put this dog out on the street. He saved my life." Jacob bit his lip and looked into his father's eyes. "If you don't want me to keep him, I'll have to—"

"Jacob, Jacob, what are you talking about? You did what you had to do to survive. Of course you can keep your little dog." Smiling, Itzak reached over and patted Quake's head.

Quake whimpered and licked Itzak's hand.

Itzak lowered his eyes. "I was the foolish one, not you. I worried our house was too small. So now we have no house. Then I worried the neighbors would complain. Now everybody in San Francisco is our neighbor! Who is going to complain about a little thing like a dog? We're all living outside like stray dogs."

Jacob looked into his father's eyes and saw himself reflected in them. A memory stirred in him. Once when he was a little boy he woke in the night and felt something soft and warm on his forehead. His father was bending over him, kissing him gently on the forehead. Jacob remembered smiling up at Papa and seeing himself reflected, safe and secure, in his father's eyes. He remembered saying "I love you, Papa" before nodding off to sleep again. Now he looked into his father's eyes and whispered the words again. "I love you, Papa."

Itzak put his arm around Jacob's shoulders. "Before the earthquake, all I could think of was your mother's death. How she adored you and Sophie! 'What am I going to do,' I asked myself over and over, 'alone in this house, without a mother for my children?'

"Oh, Jacob, I could only see how much I'd lost—not what I

still had. Then our house fell down, the city burned up, and my son disappeared. After that, the only thing that mattered was finding you." Itzak's voice cracked, and a great sob choked his words. "Now you've come back to me. Thank God. It's a miracle—both of my children are safe!"

Jacob heard a baby wail. A woman's voice began scolding, "Avi Kaufman! How many times do I have to tell you to keep the noise down? You and your brother want to holler like that? Fine, then you come rock your son to sleep."

Aunt Rose's head poked out of a tent. "How do you expect an infant to fall asleep with such a racket? Before you know it, the twins will wake up and start hollering, too." The baby's wailing got louder as Aunt Rose continued.

Avi hurried to his wife. "Shhh. Rose, look who's—"

"A dog? Noo—another dog he brings home!" She ducked out of the tent and stomped toward the fire, the baby squirming in her arms. "What's the matter with you, Avi? You think I'm running a boardinghouse for stray dogs? Haven't we got enough problems without—" Rose's stream of words came to a halt when she caught sight of Jacob. She gasped. "Oh my God! Jacob? Is that you?"

She plunked the baby in Avi's arms and grabbed Jacob's shoulders. "Where on earth did you find him?"

Jacob let her squeeze him to her chest. It was such a relief to find his family that he was even glad to see Aunt Rose.

"Jacob, Jacob, where have you been?" she asked.

"Here, in the park. I've been living with an Irish family—the Flanagans. After the earthquake, I came here with San—this boy I met in Chinatown. He got trapped when a building fell, and I helped him dig his way out."

"In Chinatown? You mean a Chinese boy?"

Jacob nodded. "I don't know what I would have done

without him. San Wei Chang. And then we met the Flanagans, Annie and Kevin. They took care of us." He looked at his father. "They're not Jewish, but—"

"Jewish, Chinese, Irish...what difference does it make?" Itzak said. "These people gave me back my son—they could be from Timbuktu for all I care! Where are they? I want to get down on my knees and thank them."

"San's not here," Jacob said. "He's in Oakland now, his father came to pick him up. But the Flanagans' tent is over that way," Jacob said. "Come on, I'll show you. I better go tell Annie where I am, anyway. She'll be worried about me."

Itzak started to follow Jacob, but he glanced at Sophie and hesitated.

"Go, Itzak, go with your son to meet these people," said Rose. "You go, too, Avi. I'll stay with the children." Rose put her hand on Sophie's head. "Sophie, better you should stay here. It's late." She said to Itzak, "I'll get her ready for bed."

"But I want to go with Jacob." Sophie's voice was a thin whine. She yawned and slipped her thumb into her mouth. "Can the doggy sleep with me, Jacob?" She put her arms around Quake's head and looked at Rose. "Auntie Rose, can the doggy sleep with me?"

Quake's whole body wiggled as he nosed Sophie's curls and licked her ears.

Rose looked at Jacob. "So this is your dog?"

Before Jacob could answer, Sophie tugged on his sleeve. "You never told me whether he's a boy doggy or a girl doggy, Jacob."

"Yes, he's my dog," Jacob told his aunt. He looked at Sophie. "He's a boy dog, Sophie, and yes, it's fine with me if he sleeps with you tonight. If Auntie Rose and Papa say it's all right."

Aunt Rose threw up her arms. "Noo—what's next? We're already sleeping outside like dogs, so now we're supposed to share our tent with a dog?" She shrugged. "Well, at least I don't have to worry about him getting dirt on my rugs!"

The baby had quieted down in Avi's arms, and Rose held out her arms to take him. Avi smiled and kissed his wife's forehead.

"Come on, Sophie," Rose said, motioning toward the tent. "Bedtime."

Sophie leaned against Jacob. "But I want to stay with Jacob." She yawned again.

"Go ahead, Sophie, you go with your aunt and get some sleep." Itzak brushed her hair out of her eyes. "Don't worry, your brother will be here when you wake up."

Jacob kissed Sophie. "Tomorrow I'm going to introduce you to Molly Flanagan. She's almost your age; you'll like her a lot. Now you better get some sleep so you won't be too tired to play."

Sophie rubbed her eyes. "Can Fluffy come, Auntie Rose?"

"Yah, why not?" she said, nudging her niece toward the tent. "Bring the dog."

Sophie looked over her shoulder. "Fluffy. Come, Fluffy."

Quake wagged his tail but didn't move. He looked at Jacob.

"Why isn't the doggy coming?"

"Fluffy is not his name, Sophie," Jacob said. "Remember, I told you that we needed to name the dog something that describes him?"

"So what do you call him?" Avi asked. "I hope it's something fancy. After all, this is the dog that saved my nephew from San Francisco's worst disaster!"

"Quake," Jacob said. "I named him after the earthquake. Because he helped me live through it."

Aunt Rose looked back over her shoulder and said, "Oy vay, if my mother in Poland could see me now. 'So this is what you wanted to come to America for?' she'd say. 'To sleep on the ground with a dog! A dog named after an earthquake, no less.'"

Jacob knelt down and stroked the dog's back. "Go, Quake. Go with Sophie. Thatta boy."

The dog padded over to Sophie, who rubbed Quake's head as she turned to follow Aunt Rose.

Jacob stood up and looked at the faces of his family. In the warm, soft light of the campfire, they seemed to glow. Uncle Avi was grinning, his kind eyes sparkling with joy. A proud, satisfied smile lit up Papa's face. It had been months since Jacob had seen his father look so happy.

At last they were together again. The awful doubts and fears were gone. For Jacob, the disaster was finally over.

AUTHOR'S NOTE

This novel takes place during the Great Earthquake and Fire of 1906 in San Francisco. The places mentioned in the story are real, and the major incidents are true. I used eyewitness accounts from survivors and photos of the wreckage to create the backdrop for my story. But this is a work of fiction, and I created all the characters (except for one—Mrs. Merrill, the wife of the head of the Red Cross).

What caused the disaster?

The earth's crust is made of giant, separate sheets of rock. (Imagine the earth as an egg and its crust as an eggshell with cracks in it.) These sheets, which are called plates, are constantly in motion. Two plates meet near California's coastline—the Pacific Plate on the west and the North American plate on the east. The 1906 earthquake was caused by these plates grinding and scraping against each other.

(To understand how the earth moves during an earthquake, put your hands together flat on a table, with your thumbs touching. Slowly slide your left hand forward while you push your right hand against your left hand. You can feel the force of your left hand as it drags forward, as well as the force of your right hand pushing. Like your thumbs, the edges of the earth's plates slide against each other, but sometimes they catch and jerk.)

The San Andreas Fault is the line where these plates touch. In the 1906 earthquake, 290 miles of this fault line ruptured and moved. (You can locate this area on a map of California by placing your finger on Mendocino County and sliding it south to Monterey County.) In some spots along the fault line, the plates moved as much as twenty-one feet relative to each other.

How much damage did the disaster do?

The Great San Francisco Earthquake began at 5:12 A.M. on April 18, 1906, and lasted less than one minute. But it caused so much damage that it's considered the worst earthquake ever recorded in the United States. People felt the tremor from southern Oregon to south of Los Angeles, and inland as far as central Nevada.

One way to compare earthquakes is by assigning them numbers on the Richter scale. This is the best-known system for measuring the magnitude, or strength, of an earthquake. Scientific instruments can detect an earthquake that measures

Ruins along Third and Market Street

Earthquake damage on Market Street

less than 3.5 on this scale, but people may not feel any movement at all. In an earthquake measuring from 3.5 up to 5, people will feel the movement, but damage will be slight. An earthquake that measures 7 and above is a major event, and damage will be extensive. The Great San Francisco Earthquake was rated around an 8 on the Richter scale.

After the big earthquake, twenty-seven aftershocks, or smaller tremors, were recorded on April 18. Most of these were mild, so they caused only a slight rocking sensation. But one of the aftershocks—the one at 8:14 A.M.—was severe enough to knock objects off tables or topple already-damaged buildings.

More than 400,000 people lived in San Francisco at the time of the Great Earthquake. Many buildings collapsed, and hundreds—perhaps thousands—of people were killed, injured, or trapped inside. When the ground shifted, gas lines and water pipes broke. Because of the leaking gas, any spark could start a fire, and that's what happened in various places around the city. One of the worst fires was started by a housewife cooking breakfast, so it's called "The Ham and Eggs Fire."

Huge crowds watch Market Street fires

Firefighters could not reach many of the fires because city streets were blocked by piles of rubble from damaged and fallen buildings. Even when their horse-drawn fire wagons managed to get to the scene, they could not douse the flames because the water pipes had broken. Small fires spread and grew, combined and intensified, until most of the downtown was destroyed. The area around City Hall was the hardest hit.

Before the earthquake, thousands of people lived in rooming houses south of Market Street, like Jacob's family. Except for Chinatown, this was the most crowded area in the city. These buildings stood on "made ground," which is swampland that people have filled in. During the earthquake, some of the buildings sank into the mud, and people drowned. Some people were still trapped in about thirty rooming houses when fires coming from three directions swept into the area. Rescuers had to abandon efforts to reach the victims, and nobody knows for sure how many people died.

The Great Fire burned for three days and three nights. It destroyed almost 30,000 buildings in about seven square miles of the city.

Since the fire also destroyed city records, we will probably never know exactly how many people were killed in the San Francisco disaster. At least 3,000 deaths have been documented, and some historians speculate that the actual death toll may be much higher.

(It's hard to grasp such large numbers, so here's a comparison that might help: About 3,000 people were killed when the Twin Towers of the World Trade Center were attacked in New York City on September 11, 2001.)

Many historians consider the Great Earthquake and Fire of 1906 to be the worst disaster caused by natural events in United States history.

What did survivors do?

With fires raging downtown and people fleeing in every direction, there was a lot of confusion. Many people were separated from their families, like Jacob and San in my story.

During the disaster, many people escaped by ferry across the bay. Later, Southern Pacific Railroad trains carried relief provisions into the city and gave survivors free tickets out of San Francisco.

Over 200,000 homeless people camped in the parks and on the streets. In Golden Gate Park, 20,000 people lived in tents. Since no fires were permitted indoors until gas lines and chimneys were repaired, everybody cooked outdoors.

What happened after the disaster?

Supplies poured into San Francisco from all over the United States—loaves of bread, drinking water, canned foods, tents, blankets, clothing, and utensils. The Red Cross, the army, and

Earthquake refugees waiting in water line

the navy contributed. The U.S. Congress appropriated $500,000 for relief.

Cleanup started immediately. By April 22, some of the city's streetcars resumed operation. Temporary refugee houses—8,000 of them, each containing six to eight families—were quickly built to replace tents and makeshift dwellings. By the fall of 1906, all of the city's inhabitants were living under roofs.

Rebuilding the major structures, such as office buildings, hotels, banks, and stores, also began quickly. In fact, nine years after the earthquake, in 1915, San Francisco held the Panama-Pacific International Exposition to celebrate the opening of the Panama Canal. When visitors arrived in the city, they were amazed that no trace remained of the Great Disaster.

Did people really discriminate against the Chinese?

Yes. At the turn of the century, prejudice against the Chinese was widespread. Mobs and labor unions drove Chinese workers out of coal mines, logging camps, factories, railroad crews, farms, and even some cities in the western states. The displaced workers were forced to live in segregated communities, called Chinatowns.

Laws discriminated against Chinese immigrants. Men who came from China to California to find work were not allowed to become citizens or send for their wives. Only wealthy Chinese merchants were permitted to bring families into this country. Chinese men were barred from marrying white women, and Chinese children were not allowed to attend California public schools.

For most San Franciscans, the Great Disaster created a "melting pot." After the quake, immigrants from different countries lived together on the streets and in the parks, sharing the same relief supplies and learning to appreciate each other's cultures. But even during the disaster, the prejudice against the Chinese continued. They were forced into separate corners of the parks, and many were afraid to get into the bread lines.

When the city began to make plans to rebuild, some prominent citizens supported a plan to relocate Chinatown outside the heart of the business district so that other businesses could have that desirable downtown property. Others wanted to prevent the Chinese who had fled to Oakland from returning to San Francisco. The Empress-Dowager of China protested this unfair treatment. After an international outcry, San Francisco's city officials were forced to restore the rightful property of Chinese citizens, and Chinatown was rebuilt in its original location.

In spite of the terrible treatment they had received, the Chinese behaved with honesty and dignity during and after the Great Disaster. Partly because of this, respect for them began to grow. Over many years the terrible prejudice against them gradually faded, and the laws that discriminated against them were overturned.

QUAKE

Where can I learn more about the Great Earthquake and Fire?

Many books and websites contain information about these events. The Virtual Museum of the City of San Francisco at *www.sfmuseum.org* is the best place to start. It includes photos, reports, and eyewitness accounts of the Great Earthquake and Fire. (You can link to this site from my website, *www.gailkarwoski.com.*)

I particularly enjoyed the clear, abundant photographs in two books: Gladys Hansen and Emmet Condon's *Denial of Disaster* (San Francisco: Cameron and Company, 1989) and Eric Saul and Don Denevi's *The Great San Francisco Earthquake and Fire, 1906* (Millbrae, CA: Celestial Arts, 1981). A wonderful photo-portrait of Chinatown can be found in John Kuo Wei Tchen's *Genthe's Photographs of San Francisco's Old Chinatown* (Dover Publications, Inc., 1984).

Young readers may enjoy Ellen Levine's brief nonfiction account in question-answer format, *If You Lived at the Time of the Great San Francisco Earthquake* (Scholastic, 1987).

Several books present the disaster through the eyes of survivors. Malcolm E. Barker's *Three Fearful Days: San Francisco Memoirs of the 1906 Earthquake & Fire* (San Francisco: Londonborn Publications, 1998) is a collection of eyewitness accounts. William Bronson's *The Earth Shook, the Sky Burned* (Doubleday, 1959) and Dan Kurzman's *Disaster! The Great San Francisco Earthquake and Fire of 1906* (William Morrow, 2001) weave eyewitness accounts into nonfiction narratives.

What other resources did you use to learn about the disaster?

In addition to the above sources, I took my information from books as well as files available at the San Francisco Public Library's History Center. Here's an alphabetical list of my other sources:

Bonnett, Wayne. *Victorian San Francisco: The 1895 Illustrated Directory*. Sausalito, CA: Windgate Press, 1996.

Burchell, R. A. *The San Francisco Irish 1848–1880*. Manchester: University Press, 1979.

Chinn, Thomas W. *Bridging the Pacific: San Francisco Chinatown and Its People*. San Francisco: Chinese Historical Society of America, 1989.

Crespi, Aurelio D. Memoir. San Francisco Public Library.

Gumina, Deanna Paoli. *The Italians of San Francisco 1850–1930*. New York: Center for Migration Studies, 1978.

Skoll, Louis. "The Jewish Race South of Market," *South of Market Journal*. April 1929.

Turner, Patricia. *1906 Remembered: Firsthand Accounts of the San Francisco Disaster*.

Walsh, James P. *The San Francisco Irish 1850–1976*. San Francisco: Irish Literary & Historical Society, 1978.

ABOUT THE AUTHOR

GAIL LANGER KARWOSKI, a former teacher of elementary, middle, and high school students, frequently returns to schools as a visiting author. She also wrote *Seaman: The Dog Who Explored the West with Lewis and Clark* and *Surviving Jamestown: The Adventures of Young Sam Collier*, a Bank Street College of Education Best Children's Book of 2001, and coauthored *The Tree That Owns Itself and Other Stories from Georgia's Past* with Loretta Hammer. Karwoski received her B.A. from the University of Massachusetts and her M.A. from the University of Minnesota, later earning an advanced elementary and a gifted teaching certificate at the University of Georgia. She lives with her family in Oconee County, Georgia.